Advance Praise

"Fans of Jane Austen will delight at this charming historical filled with romance and wit. It's not often you find a novel that wins over the many distractions of life, but this is definitely one of them. I couldn't put it down!" ~ Brielle D. Porter, Benjamin Franklin Award winner and young adult romance author of *Jester*

"Seven Days at Mannerley is a new take on historical romance with a different kind of hero and heroine. Audrey Schuyler Lancho is a fresh new voice with an unputdownable story. I loved this book and can't wait to see what she comes up with next." ~ Cindy Holby, bestselling author of *The Wind Series*

SEVEN DAYS AT MANNERLEY

Love and Lies Series, Book 1

AUDREY SCHUYLER LANCHO

Copyright ©2024 Audrey Schuyler Lancho

Cover Art Illustration copyright ©2024 Trinity McCall
Cover design © 2024 Elaina Lee/For the Muse Designs
Formatting and Interior Design by Woven Red Author Services

First Edition

Printed and bound in the United States of America. All rights reserved. No part of this book may be reproduced or transmitted in any form or by any means, electronic or mechanical, including photocopying, recording, or by an information storage and retrieval system-except by a reviewer who may quote brief passages in a review to be printed in a magazine, newspaper, or on the Web-without permission in writing from the publisher. For information, please contact Vinspire Publishing, LLC, 107 Clearview Circle, Goose Creek, SC 29445

All characters in this work are purely fictional and have no existence outside the imagination of the author and have no relation whatsoever to anyone bearing the same name or names. They are not even distantly inspired by any individual known or unknown to the author, and all incidents are pure invention.

ISBN paperback: 979-8-9880122-6-9

To Alastair and Ander, my greatest treasures.
Never stop dreaming.

PRELUDE

Dear Reader,

Let me tell you a story like no other you've ever heard, about our dear, beloved Mary Potts, and all the happenings of her remarkable life. Down the road, you will come to find out how I know all of this. But for now, let us step back in time together.

Yours truly,
Rutherford H. Wells

CHAPTER ONE

The Pub

England, 1870

For the life of her, Mary could not understand why Roy would keep scrawny, greasy Declan on staff, or why he had even hired him in the first place.

Here she found herself, yet again, dear reader, doing his chores from the previous day that were never completed, wishing her beloved brother-in-law Roy were not so very generous, and that he didn't have such a soft spot for helping people who were down on their luck.

Mary rather liked freckles and red hair—but not Declan's. He had almost doubled her work and was in no way an asset. Truly, Declan Thobbs was a painful sore on the foot of The Drabbe Inn and Pub's productivity.

Mary bent further over the basin where she labored with her teeth clenched bitterly, scrubbing a soup pot a bit harder than necessary. A pot which, of course, Declan had failed to wash after the midday meal, though it was fully his responsibility, as were the other four dirty pans waiting their turn next to the washbasin.

"Have you put on rouge, Mary Potts? Just ridiculous," her older sister Briddie interrupted her fury with the question, but the answer was implicit.

Mary didn't want to look, but in the end, she couldn't stand the heat of her sister's gaze. She met Briddie's brown eyes and olive complexion that were not at all different from her own, except for the fact that Briddie's cheeks were not artificially rosy like Mary's were tonight.

"I only tease you because I care about you. It pains me that you still allow your hope to swell against reality. Look at them. Look at *you*. It won't 'appen."

Briddie, of course, was referring to Mary's long-standing fantasy of attracting the attention of one of the fine young gentlemen who had come to dine in The Drabbe, ultimately being rescued from a life of limitations imposed on her by her sex and lowly position in life. And if she could fall in love in the process, well, even better. The cards were stacked against her, young woman as she was, and in a time that allowed only male achievement, though she knew she had an apt mind for business endeavors and all sorts of administrative tasks. Marrying up would open many doors. And for Mary, with her lowly position, quite *anything* was 'up'.

Mary Potts remained silent, though she could've said much, and rinsed another pan that pallid Declan had left in the washbasin.

"I mean, you're a *barmaid*." Briddie snorted quickly between two laughs, somewhat resembling a suckling piglet.

"I am aware," Mary retorted. "I've been one for twelve years. I'm in no need of reminding." In fact, Mary hadn't only been a barmaid in the twelve years since Briddie and Roy took her in as their own. She had worn many hats at The Drabbe Inn and Pub, with its stonework walls now speckled all over with moss and a sign so weathered by the elements that it was difficult to tell what color it had originally been painted, though it appeared to have been a sea foam green. Mary had been a laundress, repairwoman, cook, maid, rubbish lady, and of course, babysitter to the numerous children born to her sister in the same span of time, including two sets of twins.

And Mary didn't complain about the hard work; on the contrary, she was very thankful. After her mother died, she would've had no means of income in Port Lazáre as a little fatherless girl of eleven. Well, some opportunities existed, if they can be *called* that, but nothing that was not damning to her soul. In short, Roy Hicks had saved her, just like he'd rescued so many others along the way, including Declan, though this latter-mentioned fellow chose not to see it that way and did nothing productive with his second chance at life. Ah, Declan, what a coward. You'll see why.

"Why do you want to get out of here so badly?" Briddie prodded, now pouring ale in tall glasses for nicely dressed gentlemen accumulating at the pub's long bar. As they did every April, many of the rich made their way to Mannerley for the springtime ball and stopped to dine at The Drabbe, but they never stayed the night; the rooms weren't up to their standards, simple as they were. Briddie went on, offendedly, "What did we ever do to you?"

"It's not anything you've done or haven't done. I simply want to experience other things... try my hand at business and, perhaps, fall in love," Mary admitted, and Briddie huffed amusedly. "Sister, don't you remember what it was like when you were sixteen and Roy Hicks came to town and married you? Didn't you feel... rescued?"

"Aye." Briddie sighed. "But I was a silly teenage girl. I didn't know anything about being a wife or running an inn. It hasn't been quite the easiest thing in the world."

"But you had a good mind, and talents," Mary continued, "and I do, too. If I could be with a well-off man, I might also pursue a talent or passion, or—"

"Look," Briddie breathed out impatiently, leaving her work and grabbing Mary's upper arms as if quelling a toddler's tantrum. "You marrying a rich man will *never* happen.

Come," Briddie said, pulling Mary under her arm. "We'll only be a moment," she said to Roy, who now took over bartending. He grinned his endearingly goofy smirk and nodded once in affirmation, the movement jostling his feather-like blonde hair. Mary wouldn't even care if the man was as unfortunate-looking and pockmarked as Roy, if he had even half of Roy's kind heart.

Though he was only thirty-five, he was like a father to Mary more than any man had ever been. She smiled quickly at him, then Briddie pulled her to the far side of the dining room, where all the tables were bustling with fancy and hungry guests, all excited for the ball. It was, after all, one of the only socializing events in this area of the countryside before the London Season sent them all scurrying to the city to make their matches.

"Here. I want you to look about the room. Do you see anyone here that looks like they come from our class? In earnest, do you see anyone here like us?"

Mary started on one end and focused on each face, each top hat, each gentleman's coat, each lady's dress. Gold glimmered and jewels shone. Hair was coiffed; clothing was ironed; everything was perfect, as if tonight was the ball itself. But Mary knew the clothes they were wearing paled in comparison to their real outfits for the ball. Briddie was making her point, but Mary couldn't bring herself to give her the satisfaction of winning.

"I'm sure one of them could possibly take notice of me," Mary murmured obstinately.

"Mary! This fantasy ends tonight. Let me be blunt," Briddie said, scandalized, turning Mary to face her, and speaking in a lower tone. "The only luck you'd ever have with any of these men, is if one of them were to stay the night. Then the gentleman would not be so gentle with you. You'd be forgotten the next day. *None* of these men care about the working class. *None* of them are willing to give a penniless nobody a chance in terms of love. They're not even willing to buy a garment from 1869, now that it is 1870. Get your fanciful dreams out of your head. The sooner, the better."

Briddie's voice had taken on a pained gravitas. Mary sensed the anxiety she had caused her sister, and regretted it.

"Now. I've got to get back to the bar. Tend to the tables for a while."

Mary breathed against the disappointment weighing on her chest as Briddie walked away. Then she looked dejectedly around the low-beamed dining room where everything always felt sticky, at the crowd of dandies enjoying each other's company.

They were just passing through.

Not looking for love, or fate, or anything other than a good meal on their way to the Mannerley Ball. Amusement before *more* amusement. For the last twelve years, every April and October when they came through, Mary had wanted to catch a man's attention, first as a sweet-faced young pub girl for the sake of gaining praise, and later as she approached marriageable age, for the purpose of romance and self-betterment. But in those twelve years, nothing had happened. She had hoped in vain, over and over, hidden in her dull brown smock and barmaid's cap among the blandness of The Drabbe's decor.

Maybe Briddie was right. Maybe Mary would do what she had often suggested: marry a nice boy who was impoverished like herself and have enough children so someone would care for her when she was old and no longer able to work.

"But that's *Briddie's* life, not mine," Mary mumbled to herself, a bit resentful of her sister's stern reality check. Her spirit struggled to submit to the death of her dream, despite the evidence surrounding her. It was more than the death of a dream. It was resignation to be a nobody, forever. Briddie and Roy were genuinely happy that way—but Mary would not be. She needed something more.

"Miss?" a voice called. She turned on her heels, eyes wide. A middle-aged woman in a fancy hat greeted her with pursed lips. "This April air is frigid. Why is there no fire lit?"

"Oh, there is—" Mary said, but stopped as she glanced at both fireplaces, each dead.

Declan.

It was his job to stoke the fires.

Where was he anyway? He had mentioned going to retrieve something an hour ago and had never returned. No doubt he was lolling about, perhaps napping on his cot in the lean-to shanty just outside the kitchen.

"I'll light them now," Mary reassured the woman, and looked around to see many people covering up with shawls and pulling their coats tight around their collars as she scurried about to do her work—Declan's work—slightly ducking under the lowest beams.

With the first fire lit, she headed to the next, head high, breast puffed, but no one looked, just like they hadn't for the past twelve years. Her hope withered further under Briddie's dose of unwanted truth.

She slid down on her knees to kindle, but saw a metal handle out of place. After touching it lightly to make sure it was cool, she stuck her head under the fireplace and looked up. The flue was closed, also Declan's doing. He did it on rainy nights to stop the pitter-patter on the fireplace's floor, which disrupted his sleep. It would have been courteous of him to have reopened it for the next day's smoke to escape, but Declan never thought of others. It was a good thing she had seen it; otherwise, the dining room would have filled with smoke once the wood was lit.

Mary gave the flue's handle a pull. Nothing.

She braced herself on her knees and pulled with both hands. Nothing.

She realized she'd have to crawl inside the stonework structure and yank on the handle, so she took position, and, looking up to see how the thing was done, she pulled with all her might, which succeeded in opening the flue, but simultaneously released a heavy cloud of gray soot all over her, the finest particles of which coated her entirely, and clung to the dewy perspiration on her face that she'd acquired from the evening's busy dinner service.

It was immediately after this fiasco, that she noticed Declan giving into malicious laughter at her expense from the other end of the pub. His laughter was a sort of warbling, high-pitched, airy release, akin to something an old granny might produce when seeing moldy food, or like the breathy squeak of a very ugly sea-creature. Like he had never properly learned to laugh at all.

As Mary looked around, covered in soot, she realized that no one except Declan had even seen what happened, though a few fancy ladies nearby pawed at the dusty air and coughed delicately into embroidered handkerchiefs. Roy and Briddie stood further off at the bar, filling orders. Far more backs were turned to her than faces. She must matter so very little, to not even be noticed during such a great blunder. Did she really blend in so seamlessly that even the most disastrous thing went unperceived?

Desperately, she searched the gentlemen. Surely one of the fifty or so gathered would come to her aid.

But no.

They didn't care.

They would *never* care.

Briddie was right.

Out, out she ran, through the dining room, our mortified creature of gray. The dandies could make do with one fire, or lazy, sleazy, warbling Declan could light the second himself.

She exited the pub down a small corridor that connected to the inn, running out the first door on the left, tumbling through the evening penumbra onto a cobblestone terrace with a high railing around it, which was perfect for leaning on now that her grief poured out strong and the harsh sobs broke through with moans and wails.

It was official: she *was* a penniless nobody from a shady background, and would work at The Drabbe for the rest of her life, and perhaps never experience true love, and certainly never have the opportunity to combine her mind and gifts in any worthwhile endeavor. And if she were blessed enough to find love, it would be with someone poor like herself. She would never rise above her station. She would do nothing noteworthy, nothing remarkable, despite her talents, despite her skills.

She grieved what could have been, and her heart ached. She hated the fact that Briddie was right. Victorian England was a land of classes and distinctions, and Mary was born on the unfortunate side of things, in both income and gender. There was no way to rise above. There would be no rescue.

There was, in effect, no hope.

The door to the courtyard creaked open, and she turned to face her company, fully expecting Briddie or Roy to have found out what happened. She hoped for Roy. She couldn't face Briddie right now.

Instead, a tall, dark, unknown gentleman stood in the night air, seemingly unsure of what he was seeing, as he appeared to be cocking his head in curiosity, and the heavy clouds shrouding the moon didn't help his vision at all. He squinted at Mary in the dark.

"I was looking for the gentlemen's smoking room," he said, with the tiniest hint of a foreign accent, but Mary could not tell from where. "I'll just—"

"It's the next door down, if you go back in," Mary said, sniffling and turning again to lean on her railing and be melancholic for a while more until her family sought her out. The door to the courtyard shut with a creak, then a soft thud upon latching. She presumed that the dandy had found his way and that she was once again alone.

That is, until she noticed his shape near hers a moment later, leaning over the railing, just like her. She chuckled through her tears. What was this man up to? Apparently, he had gone to shut the door and come back to her side. For a moment, she feared Briddie's warning of gentlemen after dark. She certainly didn't want *that*. But the man wasted no time in putting her at ease.

"Do you normally dust yourself in a heavy gray powder before you dine?"

His voice held no derision, but a slight smile graced him. Was he trying to make her laugh?

"Chimney disaster," Mary managed to croak.

He smiled ruefully and shook his head. She could tell, though it was night, that his hair was black like hers, and his lips were plump.

"Come now," he said, warm voice speaking softly and intimately near her. "I've had many a chimney disaster, and never once have I cried over it. What's really bothering you?"

Mary had calmed down considerably. She smiled up at him through her tears. "I'm a barmaid, sir."

She said this not because it was what bothered her, but because she wanted to give him an escape; she didn't want him to think he was talking to a high-society lady who happened to be in trouble at the moment. She wanted him to understand her life was *always* hard.

"Of course... the apron. The cap. Go on," he motioned for her to proceed with his hands.

Mary admired them. They were not boyish, not at all. He had to be around her age of twenty-three, or a bit older.

Then it registered. He had told her to go on. Why would he still want to talk to her, knowing her profession? She had expected him to leave.

But he hadn't.

Mary took courage.

"I have dreams, sir. Of success, and working in a different way, and things that Victorian women are not known to do. And to be honest with you, though I fear I am speaking horribly out of place, I feel a bit stuck with my lot in life."

"I see," the man said, and after having thought a moment, he added, "I have a hard time believing that you cannot be anything you want to be."

"Why is that, sir?"

"Well, just look at me," he said, motioning up and down. "I was poor, and now, here I am."

Mary smiled. She couldn't help but feel that the man didn't understand exactly what she was going through. After all, he was a man, and in her time, men had more opportunities for success merely because of their sex. This was exactly why she wanted a man. A lady could have many doors opened easily with a powerful male by her side.

If only she were a lady and not just a pub girl.

"But you are a man," Mary protested meekly. "A man can dream and create and do. A poor woman like myself, without a man, is rather destined for stagnation."

At this, the man chuckled under his breath, then shook his head. "Don't tell me you hope to marry to escape working at this pub."

Mary's breath caught in her throat. It was exactly what she wanted. My, this man was intuitive. And he thought her plan just as ridiculous as Briddie, judging by his throaty laughter.

"Do not laugh at me, sir," Mary pleaded, gripping the iron railing tighter.

"Laugh at you? Never," he said, and then, "I only think you don't need a man to do what you want to do. You must change the way you think."

Fancy that thought. She breathed out slowly to calm her nerves. The idea of marrying up was silly, and she'd realized it, especially being faced with Briddie's facts tonight at the pub.

But was this man's idea wholly without merit?

Could it be so hard to dream of rising above, as a female, alone?

Mary thought of Myrtle, the seamstress. A business owner, who'd worked at Mannerley itself. It was true that every day the landscape for what women were allowed to do was changing. There were even campaigns to give them the vote.

A possibility, maybe.

"Thank you for your counsel, sir," Mary said politely. "You should join your friends for a smoke now. I'll be fine."

"Alright then," he said and turned to go, but then stopped and, without hesitation, took hold of Mary's hand.

The touch of her hand should not have been done, and both of them knew it, being as they were in private and in the dark. But perhaps because of the forbidden nature of the contact, Mary tingled all over, like she never had before, as if a strange force coursed through her, and her face flushed hot beneath the layer of clingy soot. He must have felt the mysterious energy too because he cocked an eyebrow and tilted his head with intrigue.

He spoke again. "I'll go. Only promise me you will not stop dreaming. And that you won't rely on a man to make those dreams come true."

She was sure her soul was intertwining with his as his flesh rested against hers. To her amazement, he brought her hand to his soft mouth, and ever so lightly, kissed the back of it, leaving it cool in the nighttime breeze. She shuddered out a heavy breath. She could *never* stop dreaming now.

"I promise, Mr..."

"Singh," he said, releasing her hand, and walking to the courtyard door that led back inside the establishment.

"Like a song?" Her voice was breathy, immature.

"*S-i-n-g-h*. It's a surname. From India." His amused smile flashed in the dark.

With that, he disappeared into The Drabbe, and Mary's hope rose victoriously from the ashes in which it had died only moments before.

CHAPTER TWO

The Trunk

It was the next morning, Thursday, April 7, 1870, when the serendipitous events had their start and came one after another, in such a way as to alter the course of many lives, up to hundreds with the passage of time. You can trust old Rutherford on this…

Mary woke that morning feeling that something indeed was different. How could she have escaped this feeling? After all, she had met Mr. Singh. And just because of that, everything had now changed.

The swallows chirped from their nests in the eaves outside her room on the top floor of the inn. As she did every morning, she changed the soiled Hicks babies snuggled soundly on the blankets on the floor. She woke the older children to care for the tiny ones, and then glided through her other morning chores, oozing optimism and giddiness.

He had smiled at her; he had wanted to make her laugh. And the way he stopped and held her hand... Oh, she shouldn't have. But she was glad she did. The tingle was unlike anything she had ever experienced. She didn't know how, but she had to find this captivating, scintillating, perfect Mr. Singh. He had kissed her hand, even with her covered in soot and dressed as a pub girl. What more would he do when he saw her with her black curls loose and healthy complexion on display?

When she got down to the kitchen to brew the coffee and boil the eggs, Declan was there acting like his usual self as he kneaded dough for bread.

"This is *women's* work. You're late, and it's not fair for a man to be subjected to this. I'll make it known how I feel 'bout it. They're always making me do humiliatin' work. I'll tell them, alright." Declan always boasted retaliation or rebellion but never followed through. He was as spineless as he was listless.

"Don't worry. I'll do it," Mary said, trying to sound neutral in order to hide the excitement that had sprouted in her heart.

He snatched her hands with his pale, clammy ones. "No, not today. You've got soot under your nails still, and they'll blame *me* if the bread is gritty. Just like they blame me for everything. Although, the trouble I got in last night was worth seeing you covered in ash. What a show you put on!" At this, Declan laughed, and Mary noticed his teeth were a shade darker than his skin.

"As long as it brought you joy, Declan," Mary mumbled under her breath, and walked past him toward the back shanty to fetch the eggs.

When she walked in, Roy was there with everything needed for breakfast on a tray about to head to the kitchen. He set it down, straightened himself, and wiped his bony hands on his apron. "I've got it covered, sister," he said, referring to breakfast, with compassion in his eyes. Oh, dear. Roy must have thought she was depressed after the embarrassing fireplace debacle from the night before.

"I'm fit to work, Roy," she said, still keeping her emotions in check. She couldn't give away her secret hope of Mr. Singh yet. She would rather tell Roy than Briddie, who would just laugh at her, but she wanted to wait it out a while and make sure her feelings continued before disclosing. To Mary's advantage, she was very skilled at hiding her feelings and acting a different way than she really felt, without anyone noticing. She had learned at an early age that if she acted too excited her dreams would get shot down, and she'd be reminded that she was a poor little nothing born in shame. In contrast, if she acted too depressed and forlorn, she'd be derided for having a pity-party and told to keep her chin up, or else. The consequences were never abusive, just extra chores and such. This frequent emotional concealment had made her a potentially excellent theatre actress.

"Now, now," he said, patting her on the head as if she were one of his tiny tots. "Last night was hard for you. You went about dinner service completely distracted. I know you, Mary, and I could tell you had something on your mind that consumed you. I think you should take the morning off. Or perhaps do a chore you enjoy. I've said my piece, now go." This last part was announced with mock bravado; Roy could never be harsh. Briddie wore the disciplinary trousers.

So, with newfound freedom, Mary went about her morning unsure of what to do with herself, at times scrambling about doing things she normally couldn't do, like tidying her own bed and belongings, or talking a bit more leisurely with the older children, rather than laying out orders for them.

About mid-morning, she remembered that she had not yet picked through the rubbish heap, which was a chore she generally enjoyed, so she headed that way. And being as it felt like such a very *different* day, she slid off her barmaid cap and let her dark curls topple out and down her slender back. Even if she were going to pick through trash, she was fully alive and freer than ever, and she might as well be pretty doing it. If only Mr. Singh could see her *now*.

Once there, she rolled up her sleeves and inspected the recent piles of discarded items and household trash brought from town to The Drabbe, toppling over heavier items with a large rod to see them better. She had learned not to use her hands unless the item was truly salvageable. Whenever a person dumped behind The Drabbe, they paid Roy a penny or two, money that was used to hire a boy to load up wagons and haul it to the gorge. Before that was done, of course, Mary did her sorting job. The things people threw away were surprising, and there was always a great variety of rubbish, since many wealthy people passing through discarded all manner of broken, stained, or otherwise useless items and clothing.

Mary prodded at a pile, which dislodged and splayed its items out for her scrutiny. With her stick she quickly tossed a few cans and broken crates to the side, but chose to pick up a child's play dress, soiled at the hem and ripped in the back, draping it over her left arm as she continued to hunt through the rubbish. Ugh, used bandages. Disgusting. Then there were potato peels and eggshells on top of an old moth-eaten velvet curtain; that certainly wasn't worth the trouble of cleaning and mending.

But under the curtain, a gleam of bronze caught her eye. She tossed her rod and the play dress over to the clearing, and quickly, and a bit fearfully of dump critters, she grabbed two clean spots of the heavy curtain and slung it away, hard as she could. There, at the very bottom of the pile, was a new, leather portmanteau-style traveling trunk with bronze clasps and large, gilded initials, A. R.

Mary grabbed the handle and dragged it over to the clearing, plopping her rump on the ground. The chest was heavy, and definitely full of something. Her spirits lifted at the prospect of perhaps having found something good. "Let's see what's inside," she said as she undid the clasps and tried to open it by tugging at the top handle.

Locked.

She hmphed. Then it occurred to her that Roy would know what to do, so she dragged it toward the back door of the kitchen, where she knew Roy would be overseeing the breakfast service with freckled Declan Thobbs.

～

"Ah!" Declan shouted dramatically, almost spilling the tray of coffee he had just prepared. "You little devil!"

Roy emerged from the storage room shanty. "What is it? What's happened?"

"This child of yours came out from under the cupboard and startled me and almost ruined the coffee service. I swear, this place is absolutely *crawling* with babies!"

Roy laughed a bit, assuming Declan was making a play on words. When he realized he meant it negatively, he grew serious. "Yes, we have a few of them."

"Well, I wish you'd had less," Declan exclaimed, angrily.

"Ah, is that so?" Roy asked, now growing heated. "And which of my beloved children would you like to extinguish, exactly?"

"We could start with that one that almost burned me to death with this boiling brew, then move on to the nursing twins who keep me up with their cries when I'm trying to sleep." Declan repositioned his tray for service, assuming his negativity would be given a pass, as it always was.

Mary opened the door to the kitchen, breathless, having dragged the heavy luggage up by herself. Not taking time to read the situation, she started her announcement, "I have found a—"

"Declan Thobbs, you will pack your things and be gone today," Roy bellowed and looked at Declan red-faced, chest heaving. "Not another word!" Roy shouted, as Declan attempted to speak.

Declan, deeply offended, pressed his pallid hand to his chest. His mouth formed a letter o. Then his brow furrowed, and he stomped to the back room of the kitchen, slung his few things into a cloth bag, and stomped through the dining room, dodging low-lying beams as he went. He then barged out the establishment's front door, which he shut with a dramatic slam.

Mary, noticing Roy was upset, patted his shoulder in consolation.

"It's alright," Roy reasoned. "He's a thief anyway. Better off without him."

"Now, Roy, how could you keep him if you knew he was stealing?"

"Didn't Jesus keep Judas around? I follow the Good Lord's example."

"Truly, your heart is bigger than your head," Mary said.

"Now, my sister," Roy said, turning his attention to Mary. "What did you say you had found? Forgive me; I was flustered."

Mary led Roy to the trunk as the baby crawled into the dining room, babbling.

"A trunk. It's locked."

"Oh, my. Probably empty, you know. The rich, if something seems broken or out of style, they just chuck it. We'll sell it. I'll give you part of the sale."

"No, no. It's full. I can tell."

Roy gave the suitcase a nudge and confirmed that it was quite heavy. He looked at Mary, his face contorted into an innocent, excited smile. He had her wait there and went to fetch his oldest boy to finish up breakfast service in Declan's absence and prepared the tubs for wiping the tables before lunch. Then he told Mary to get one end, and he got the other, and they carried the trunk easily between the two of them, up the narrow wood steps of the inn and into Briddie and Roy's own room in the attic. Briddie was taking a break from her mid-morning work of laundering and ironing to feed the babies and tots that still nursed. She remarked she was missing one, and Roy ran out quickly, returning with the chubby crawler that had startled Declan.

"Now, I know they're here somewhere," he said, referring to his tools. The room was jam-packed with crates and boxes, not poorly organized, but the quantity of things made the system difficult to be effective when in a hurry. "Aha! Here," he said, emerging from under the bed with dust bunnies on his fluffy blond hair. He had a chisel in one hand and a mallet in the other.

He set to work cracking into the lock. Briddie dropped the babies off in the other room with Roy's old mother. She came back in and locked the door behind her and opened her curtains wide, so the mid-morning sun came gliding in, illuminating all three of them on the floor around the trunk. With a final blow of the mallet, the lock popped loose and the three of them looked at one another in excited anticipation.

"Go on, open it," Roy urged Mary. "You found it. Or maybe it found you." Briddie and Roy smiled goofily, eyes wide, nodding.

Mary obeyed, lifting the top of the portmanteau and displacing the packing paper that covered what appeared to be garments. Roy and Briddie gasped in delight as Mary pulled out the finest violet ball gown she had ever seen. It practically sparkled. She stood and held it up to herself. "Have you ever seen anything like it?" she asked, in awe. "Not even the finest gentry girls have dresses like this. Oh, this will fetch a fine sum."

Briddie clapped. "Try it on," she squealed with delight.

Mary slid it on right over her clothes and impersonated a rich girl, her dark lashes fluttering and hips swaying as many a snooty woman was known to do. She waved around her face with an imaginary fan, and Briddie tossed her a real one from A. R.'s trunk.

"No need to fake it," Briddie laughed, then said to Roy, "Just look at all this." She and Roy emptied the trunk one item at a time, neatly folding the garments after admiring them with Mary. A night dress, two petticoats, another blue, less formal dress, a green everyday dress, a straw hat with silk flowers, stockings, a corset, and two fine leather boots that looked to be rather large. Indeed, whoever this girl was, she was tall and had huge feet. The dress crumpled on the floor under Mary's average-height frame.

"Who on earth would throw this away?" Briddie asked to no one in particular, fingering the fine silk flowers on the hat.

"I doubt it was thrown away. Rather... lost," Roy suggested. "What's that?" He asked as the women went through the items, giggling, imagining, and speculating how much each thing would bring when sold.

He fetched a brown envelope with a broken wax seal from the very bottom of the trunk and held it with trepidation, perhaps fearing it contained information about A. R. and thus the moral obligation to return the costly items to their owner, or perhaps because he had an inkling of what the letter really was.

Mary and Briddie stopped their silly play and looked at each other, and at the envelope. Mary snatched it, opened it, and read. Her face grew warm, and her eyes grew wide.

"It's an invitation," Mary said, now breathless, "to the springtime ball at Mannerley on Saturday, April 9, at seven in the evening. It's addressed to Agnes Riboneaux."

Briddie clasped both hands over her mouth, and Roy gasped in surprise.

"You have to go," Briddie said, eyes wide, seemingly surprised she was even saying those words.

Indeed, Mary couldn't believe her stick-in-the-mud sister was encouraging it. "No, no," Mary protested, "I couldn't."

"But you *must*."

"The Drabbe is always packed the day of the ball. There's no way I could."

"Briddie's right. You must go. You simply must. We'll make do," Roy said.

"But it's wrong. This is another girl's invitation. What will poor Agnes do?"

"Oh, darling, I'm sure she's already written to procure a replacement. A girl rich as 'er," Briddie said while tracing the gilded letters on the trunk with her finger. "Well, this won't be a worry to her. But to a girl as poor as you, this is an experience and a chance you will only get one time. And this is that time."

"I just couldn't. I would feel too guilty. I'll stay here. We can get the items back to this girl. We can send word to the staff at Mannerley that it's in our possession. She'll need only to stop by and get it."

At this, Roy placed his hand on Mary's, as she was now slumped on the floor with both of them around the trunk. "Mary, my dreams have flown the nest. I will never, ever get an opportunity like this one. Neither will my Briddie, nor will my children, most probably. *You're going.* And you'll enjoy every minute of it. And it will be our secret. The belongings can be returned to Miss Agnes after the ball, no harm done."

Mary thought it over and looked back and forth at her sister and brother-in-law so hopeful, so innocent, the best parents to her without even being her parents. How she loved them, even when they were hard on her, and even when Briddie behaved like a bucket of cold water. How she admired them.

"Live your dreams, just for one night," Briddie urged, shiny tears gathering around the bottom rims of her eyes. "You've waited twelve years for something like this. I stand by what I say, it won't happen here at The Drabbe, not in a million years. But at a *ball*..." Briddie smiled sweetly.

Suddenly, the memory of Mr. Singh and his secret courtyard touch flooded Mary's mind. He hadn't indicated that he was going to the ball. Of course, they hadn't talked very much. But he was passing through at the correct time to be a guest at the ball, in the dining room full of other people headed there, as they did every April. But then again, he could be going as one of the many streetside spectators of the pomp, and not as an invitee at all. He *had* said he used to be poor. It wasn't likely that he was now invited by someone at Mannerley. And he was a foreigner, at that.

But what if he *were* there? What if she could actually dance with him? Even if she had to come back to The Drabbe the day after to pick up where she left off, a dance with Mr. Singh might fill her heart with such joy she could live out her days as an old spinster satisfied forever with the excitement of that one memory alone.

Or perhaps it would inspire her as he had charged her—to never stop dreaming and to fight for those dreams herself. Living the impossible for just one night might be the medicine her longing heart needed.

At any rate, she'd be closer to her dream than ever before, in circumstances where she might be noticed.

This thought, paired with Briddie's and Roy's imploring eyes, finalized her decision.

"Well," Mary said, keeping her outward emotions in check, "I suppose I could go as Agnes. As you say, it's only one short night."

At this, Roy and Briddie erupted in excited exclamations and raised Mary up off the floor for a quick dance around the room, with Briddie singing God Save the Queen loudly and off-key and Roy twirling them around triumphantly, his boots tapping rhythmically on the creaky wooden floors.

CHAPTER THREE
The Arrangements

"We're all rootin' for ya, Mary," said Myrtle, the seamstress of Hembin, with pins in her mouth as she planned out the finishing stitches on the hem of the fancy violet dress.

It was the evening of Friday, April 8, the day before the ball, and Mary was preparing in both physical and intangible ways. She needed a ball gown alteration, but she also needed information. And she knew Myrtle was the one to give it, town gossip as she was.

The ballgown now fit Mary Potts' slender physique like a fine glove, of which she—or Agnes—also had two, each adorned with a small pearl clasp and a cuff of lace. She tried on this ensemble with Briddie in the shop like a regular gentlewoman, but Myrtle knew better. Even so, she did not ask how they got the clothes, and Mary wasn't giving details.

Myrtle and Briddie had helped each other so much through the years that they had developed a very trusting alliance. Myrtle would talk about anyone, and pry anywhere––except where Briddie and her family were concerned. There, she didn't meddle. She was extremely loyal. Mary didn't know the details of how Briddie had helped her, but she figured it must have been something substantial to give birth to such a strange and faithful symbiosis.

Whatever had happened between them, Mary was thankful for it. Because she needed to know how to act out her role at the ball. Someone had invited Agnes to it. Who could it have been? And why?

She watched Myrtle working on the hem, making tiny stitches with gold thread, and tried to think of the right way to ask the questions that she desperately needed answered. Luckily an opportunity arose almost immediately.

"Finished! Turn round to the looking glass," Myrtle instructed, stepping behind Mary and Briddie so they could admire the look.

The flowing skirts, embellished in gold thread, draped down from under the bodice and adorned the floor like an overturned flower, with a slight bustle starting at the small of her back, which was attractively accentuated. The dress's fitted bodice contained a row of gilded buttons along the middle, and a sort of velvet jacket that extended about three-fourths of the way down her arms. The jacket was not able to be closed, leaving the bodice and its buttons visible, as well as just the slightest curvature of the top of Mary's bosom.

"Don't be embarrassed, dear; it's fine to give a man an idea of the goods that come with the purchase price." Myrtle said this in a quiet and sultry voice. She was definitely entering into gossip-mode. "Besides," Myrtle continued, "this slight decolletage is nothing compared to the revealing frocks I saw women wear as a little girl back in the 1820s. Those dresses would certainly make the queen blush."

Mary smiled at this statement but bit her tongue. She would never divulge that she was quite proud of the way she looked, bosom and all, and that she had not espoused the popular prudishness of the era.

"Have you ever been to a ball, Myrtle?" Mary asked impishly, taking advantage of the subject to fish out what she needed. She couldn't imagine a young Myrtle in ball attire; the fifty-something woman only ever wore black. Widow's weeds, no doubt.

"One or two. *But...*" Myrtle pounced, ready to spill, "I was seamstress for a spell for Lady Blanche Huntron herself, the owner of Mannerley. I've got stories. But I'm sure you don't want to hear about that." Myrtle smirked and raised an eyebrow, taunting Mary to pry.

And Mary gave in. "Oh please, tell me. After all, I'll meet her tomorrow."

Myrtle clasped Mary's hands and pulled her closer, slightly hunching. She darted her eyes to each side before talking again. "I don't know if meeting her is a good idea," she warned, even lower in tone.

Briddie, noticing the tittle-tattle about to take place, announced she needed a moment to look for something for Mary. Myrtle waved her off flippantly with her hand and Briddie exited and jogged across the street, weaving in-and-out of the train of carriages that clogged the road, all heading to Mannerley for the festive weekend.

"Why ever not, Myrtle?" Mary said, egging her on.

"Because, darling. Let's be frank. You're not going as *yourself*, now, are you? You're going as another." One side of Myrtle's mouth rose in a would-be smile.

"You've caught me," Mary said.

"So, you can't meet Lady Huntron. You must avoid her. To be invited, you must be personally acquainted with her, meaning whoever you are taking the place of is someone that she has already met in her life."

"I see," Mary said. "If she sees me, she might realize I'm not who I say I am."

"Precisely!" Myrtle exclaimed. "Though, there *is* the chance she wouldn't remember your looks, even if she did remember to invite you. She's eighty-three, last I heard. She's looking a bit like a skeleton. They say her pallid skin hangs off her face like a drape. She grows more scatter-brained each year, and flits into a delusional frame of mind that makes her behave as in her youth during the regency era, like some dreadfully out-of-place Jane Austen character."

Myrtle's raspy voice descended into a derisive chuckle. "Each one of these spells makes her long for youthful company, so if she remembers names or has written them somewhere, she sends out invitations to her ball and fills her guest rooms with young faces. And this time, *you* are one of those young faces."

Now, Mary was getting somewhere.

"And is she married?"

"Oh, child. Her personal matters are another tale entirely. Lady Huntron was a socialite, daughter of a wealthy duke, and she married an untitled gentleman named John Prickwhile. He was viewed with great esteem due to his booming industries in India. It is said he produced tea and textiles, but whether this is true or not escapes me. At any rate, she and this Prickwhile never had their own children, as it was said Lady Huntron wore her undergarments too tight, though this was well before the corset era.

"They were known to lavish their affections on the gentleman's nephew, Robert Prickwhile, and when dear Robert died suddenly in 1850—the same year I got my seamstress position at Mannerley—they doted on his children, which were their great-niece and great-nephew, and the heirs to Mannerley estate. They were beautiful children, and delightful—nothing like their mother, Daphne. They're in their twenties by now. John Prickwhile died in 1855, and left Lady Huntron everything he owned, including Mannerley."

"But why is her name now Huntron?"

"Ah, yes. While I was working for her, she briefly remarried to her namesake Lord Huntron, but procured a divorce for undivulged reasons. But *I* know what happened better than anyone—"

"I'm back!" Briddie announced, cutting off Myrtle's gossip, and trotting through the open door. She shut it loudly behind her, a bundle under her left arm.

Mary and Myrtle exchanged smiles. "I shall tell you some other time. You'll do fine, lass," Myrtle said, pinching her cheek.

Mary was surprised to see that Myrtle's eyes were glistening with nostalgia, but she didn't have time to ask her why; Briddie's excitement demanded Mary's attention.

"Look what I've brought," Briddie said, presenting Mary with a lumpy cloth bag. Mary promptly opened it with a feisty smile, not knowing what to expect. Inside were Briddie's own black silk wedding shoes from twelve years before. They were a bit out of style, but they were much better than Agnes's fine leather boots, which were almost a foot long. Mary remembered her mother taking money from the jar behind the bookshelf, her secret money, and dragging little Mary along to the bigger shops in Port Lazáre. With the shamefully-earned sum, she bought the shoes and a matching black silk hat for her eldest daughter, ignoring the sourpuss clerks who treated them as inferiors. The hat Briddie had sold when she was in a pinch. But the shoes—one could *always* use fine shoes. If Mary's mother could see her now. How she would laugh that deep gypsy cackle and grab her chin and smile into her face.

"Thank you, Briddie," Mary said, and her emotions rose from her heart to her moistening eyes. "I will return them safe and sound."

"What's the fun in that? Ruin them. Give them a good run. Lose them in an episode of passion!" Briddie smiled wildly, and Myrtle laughed.

Briddie hugged her sister, then excused herself, and headed back to the pub to prepare for the dinner service.

Myrtle instructed Mary to undress behind a screen, and when she needed help with her corset, Myrtle obliged.

"You know, Myrtle," Mary confessed quietly, suddenly nervous, "I met a gentleman at the pub. He kissed my hand. Do you think he could be there? Do you think I might fall in love?"

Myrtle suddenly stopped loosening the laces, as if she had to think very carefully how to answer.

"Well, Mary, what does your sister say about it?"

"She already told me to live my dreams for just one night; to experience how the rich live. But if she knew about the gentleman I already met at The Drabbe, I know what she *would* say. That there's no chance for anything lasting, and to dream no further than the excitement and experience of the ball."

Myrtle became uncharacteristically quiet. When she spoke again, her tone was sad, not gossipy, not derisive. Mary suspected that Myrtle's mysterious loyalty to Briddie was now in play.

"I'm sorry my dear," she said. "I'm afraid your sister is right. You must go to enjoy yourself for just one night. Not to befriend anyone, or fall in love, or make some bloke love you. You must go as a ghost, and then come back to The Drabbe on Sunday, ready to slip back into your normal life. Never mind this rich young man that showed you attention. Forget him. It is the only way you will not get hurt."

Mary put on her own garments, carefully boxing the fine things she would wear to the ball the following day. She thanked Myrtle, and she meant it because she knew both Myrtle and Briddie were trying to protect her. Much as it pained her, she forced herself to tone down her dreams and accept that Mr. Singh was just a courtyard happenstance. She would not see him again, and she could not make any ties with anyone. She would enjoy the experience for the night, and that was all.

The day arrived, and the time arrived, and Mary, now fully dressed, accessorized, combed, pinned, and painted, grabbed her fan, and asked Briddie how she looked. They both squealed and jumped about before Mary stopped to stare into her mirror. She was a vision in violet. The curves of the corset made her fully a woman if she hadn't been before. The fabric comfortably hugged her hips, and her flat buttoned belly ran up like a stem, blossoming at the top with the curvature of her breasts. Her cheeks flushed at seeing herself in such a way, and the rosiness was even more becoming to her face. Her black curls were pinned without expertise but were accidentally very fashionable.

Briddie interrupted her self-admiration. "Yes, yes. This will do."

Then Briddie rushed her off to the carriage behind the Drabbe. Of course, Roy was also dumbstruck at seeing his young sister-in-law so elegant. He may have been nervous for her because he was oddly quiet during the two-hour carriage ride to Mannerley Town, though he gave her a small and awkward talk about male intentions. She couldn't help but giggle as Roy played father.

Her nervous excitement made time fly by. Soon, she could tell through the small back window that they were arriving in the hill country that Mannerley was famous for. As they clopped along, the enormous, colonnaded white house of Mannerley Estate sharpened into view. Every spring-blooming flower flanked Mannerley along with the quaint resort town that had popped up all around it.

Mary held her face near the window in disbelief. It was all so lovely. There were luxurious inns and apartments and shops geared toward all manner of exercise and leisure. Mary imagined young, rich visitors starting their days with long walks on the grounds, as there appeared to be many well-maintained paths. Later on, she fancied that they might split into groups by sex, with men going riding, fishing, or hunting, and women doing various indoor activities, or perhaps resting under the shade of trees. The kinds of things they would do were foreign to a working girl such as herself—needlepoint or music lessons.

In the evenings after supper, perhaps the groups would reunite for evening chats on the veranda, charades, card games, reading aloud, or any other sort of merriment that suited their fancy. Of course, there was also archery, croquet, and cricket. So many fun things existed with such little time to complete them all. Then at nightfall, Mary mused, they would all return to their rented rooms and perhaps the next day visit the gourmet shops that offered their services in Mannerley Town, eating chocolate bonbons and trying on brand new silk hats and gloves.

Oh, what a life. And what a gift, to be able to experience it, if only for one night.

Roy drove behind the jewelry shop and stopped there, being as the carriage was very old and he did not want to risk Mary's fake reputation by having her be seen arriving in a dilapidated old junker with mismatched parts.

Roy dismounted quickly and scurried to open Mary's door just as she was climbing out. "No, no! Shut it! Shut it!" he said, playing stern. She laughed, and obeyed, and he opened the door and extended his hand to help her down, bowing exaggeratedly like a French palace footman, missing his powder blue coattails and white wig. Mary cackled, not unlike her mother, and then took both of Roy's hands, as he looked into her face like a proud father.

"You're entirely becoming. Every bit of the ensemble. You're just like a precious flower."

"How can I thank you?" Mary asked, feeling herself growing sentimental. "You did this, all of this."

"Enough, enough." Roy sniffed deep and blinked back tears. His bulbous nose grew red with emotion. "Do you have the invitation? And the fan? Your gloves?"

"Yes, I have. I have it all."

"Well, then," Roy laughed forcedly as one does when trying not to cry. "Go on, then. Live this magic. I'll be waiting here for you. I imagine these things last through the night, so return here when you will. I never need much sleep, anyway."

"Oh, Roy, my brother." Mary hugged him tight, then surveyed her surroundings and traipsed up a stone walk between some shops. She waved goodbye to Roy, and stepped out onto the main road into an unknown society as an unknown person.

CHAPTER FOUR
The First Day

"You'll not befriend anyone," Mary whispered, repeating Myrtle's words to herself and keeping her plan straight. She struggled up Mannerley's gravelly front drive in Agnes's ball gown and Briddie's silk heels, dodging horse droppings and weaving around carriages that approached to drop off their guests at Mannerley's front doors. It wasn't exactly easy to trudge up a walk and give oneself a pep talk in such a tight corset.

"You're only here as a ghost, for one night, never to be seen again. You mustn't draw attention to yourself or entertain too much, lest someone try to keep a friendship with you." And what had been the last thing Myrtle had said? Ah, yes: "And you mustn't fall in love or cause some bloke to love *you*."

"You there," a male voice called, and Mary looked sharply to her left. "Yes, you! Won't you ride with us, and along the way we may become friends?"

It was an impossibly handsome, golden-haired man leaning out of a white carriage, extending his hand her way.

Me? She thought to herself, having briefly forgotten she no longer looked like a scrubby waitress. *Oh, yes, me!* She impulsively decided that perhaps it would not be the worst problem to befriend someone and receive a little attention, and she slung her hand tightly into the young man's warm grip, and he in turn hauled her up into the carriage where she squeezed herself in on the upholstered leather bench seat across from him and another young lady who was smiling brightly and sporting a nice burgundy taffeta gown. "I thank you."

"In truth, I was worried for your hemline, so I coaxed my brother into offering you a ride," said the girl with mousy brown, limp hair under a fine silk hat, and clear blue eyes. "Antoinetta," she said, extending her gloved hand and shaking Mary's.

"Charmed." Antoinetta had a face that smiled even when she wasn't. "I'm Mary," spoke our protagonist, and her cheeks instantly burned. She was supposed to say Agnes. "Mary Riboneaux." She wondered if the name sounded as false to them as it did rolling off her own tongue. "And the man whose hand I took?"

"Arthur Prickwhile," he said and bowed what he could inside the small cabin as they bumped along.

Indeed, they were so close that she had to cross her legs and her floating foot rested on the opposite bench seat between Arthur's seated frame and the door of the carriage.

"I am heir to this fine estate, along with my sister, and here for a short visit from my home in Calcutta, India. And I must add, grateful to take a hand soft as yours."

Mary stifled a chuckle, as this flirtation seemed to her wholly contrived. Her hands were rough from a decade of washing and serving, though Agnes's silk gloves did a fine job at hiding the fact. Even though she was now in the presence of a rich young heir and heiress, and because of this was a bit nervous, she was able to keep her acting in check because she knew she looked the part. She made a joke to ease along the conversation. "So, as it were, you are Ant and Art Prickwhile?"

The two fine young ones looked at one another, smiles brimming, then burst into laughter. "We've never been called such, but the thing is playful," Antoinetta said and then, "Where do you come from Mary? And why were you walking? I know nothing of you; indeed, your name is wholly unfamiliar to me."

"Bah! As if it were to be familiar, sister. When you're only here three or four months out of the year. And who is to keep up with all of Lady Huntron's young obsessions these days, there are *so* many." This said Arthur Prickwhile, organizing his cravat. "But my sister is right, who are you, and have you no chaperone?"

"No." An unmarried young lady should've had a chaperone. There was simply no excuse. Mary looked around the carriage for some clue, panicking and praying inside her head. "Chaperones are not required in—" Just then she saw a carriage passing and caught the first two letters, GR, on the name printed atop. "In Greece. Where I'm from." *Oh, you foolish girl. Greece, a place of which you know nothing.* Why hadn't she just said Spain? Her mother always suspected a Spanish sailor named Carlos had been her father because Mary had his eyes, and her mother never forgot anyone's eyes. Mary had read and learned a bit about Spain since then; it certainly wouldn't have been as much of a lie as Greece. She secretly pinched her own arm in punishment.

"I say! You do look Greek, what with the complexion and the curls. And I'm glad to know this revived puritanism has not extended to the Mediterranean zones, I do loathe it so. As if a young woman were incapable of managing herself around others. Now, let me, it's rudimentary, and it's been years, but I will try," Arthur distorted his handsome face as he asked her some basic Greek question, *Pos-E-say*, it sounded to her.

"Oh, no, I don't speak it. I was raised in an English settlement." Too many lies, in such a short elapsing of time. Mary wondered how to keep it all straight. This carriage ride was testing the dexterity of her mind.

"But the surname, is that not French?" Antoinetta asked.

"It is," Mary said and abruptly stopped talking with a smile, giving fewer details, and thus having fewer lies to keep up with, resolving to be more mysterious. She wondered if the Prickwhiles would be satisfied.

"Delightful!" Antoinetta turned to her brother, who was glaring, quite obviously enamored, at Mary. "An international, multicultural girl!"

"Yes, yes," Arthur said smoothly, not taking his hazelnut eyes off Mary. "But it's too bad she's cruel and had me speaking Greek for the first time since my New Testament school days. She might have told me before that she didn't speak it and saved me the shame."

"Oh, I do apologize sir," Mary said earnestly, not wanting to offend. He laughed and said it was all in jest, and then she felt his hand secretly caress the top of her foot through her stocking, well out of his sister's view. She looked his way, and he met her gaze. His eyes didn't budge, and a small mischievous smile lifted one side of his mouth as his greenish-brown eyes narrowed to a squint. Mary's heart started hard, and she pulled her foot away, which made his smirk widen out to a pearly grin. This man was dangerous; she felt it all over.

"Well, Mary Riboneaux of Greece," Antoinetta announced as the carriage stopped in front of Mannerley's grand entryway. "You shall be my special friend tonight, as the friend I have here with me is not of the social type, and I don't know any of the girls about here."

They were let down by the footman, Arthur followed, and they made their way through the enormous front doors to the reception, where Arthur joined his gentlemen friends at the bottom of the grand staircase.

Mary tried her hardest not to die of wonder at the most stunning architecture and décor she had ever seen. She stood in the foyer on solid polished marble. A collection of fine Chinese vases added color to the dark wood and complimented the red velvet carpet of the grand staircase, and there were portraits galore. Down a large hallway to the right of the staircase, Mary could make out a floral-themed room behind double glass doors. Everything, everything was perfect and beautiful.

Antoinetta was chatting away, having taken her arm, and Mary almost didn't hear her, absorbed as she was with the surroundings. "... but when all of this becomes ours, I may move here permanently, and perhaps secure a marriage with the fellow I love after he finishes studying the law. Although now, I am in no rush to do so, having many friends in Calcutta and the lucrative business and my brother to look after me.

"Lady Huntron called us here to stay one month ago, expecting she may die any day—she is such a dramatic old bat. I keep telling her she must wait to die until I'm ready to resettle in England." Antoinetta laughed and realized Mary was only half-listening. "Mary? Oh yes, it's lovely, isn't it? I'll show you all of it later. Perhaps tomorrow. Come now." And then, approaching a neatly dressed servant, she said, "This is Mary Riboneaux. Please take her jacket and her invitation."

"I'll give nothin' of the sort!" Mary blurted without thinking, almost too near her real accent.

"Why ever not, Mary?" Antoinetta asked, quite perplexed.

Mary pulled herself together, thinking on her feet. "The jacket is part of my ensemble, and the invitation I had hoped to keep as a souvenir." The truth, of course, was that she wanted less evidence of her wrongs against Agnes in other people's hands.

Antoinetta laughed sweetly. "My dear friend, I take it that there is not much high society in Greece. Your high-collared velvet jacket is a staple of afternoon wear, and this is an evening event, you see. And the invitations are necessary to collect. After all, I am the one burdened with mailing letters of gratitude to all our guests for their presence tonight. I would hate to overlook sending you a letter. See how many hundreds are here? I shall never remember all of them on my own. Not to worry, I will get you a better souvenir." She spoke all this while removing Mary's jacket to reveal two velvet cuffs that hung across her upper arms, leaving her shoulders bare.

She read the invitation as she handed it off to the servant. "Oh," she remarked, befuddled. "This says Agnes."

"Oh, does it?" Mary thought quickly. "It's my middle name."

"Well then, there's been a confusion, Mary Agnes. My apologies. Come along, it's almost seven."

Antoinetta rushed her straight through the immaculate entryway toward the back of the house and into the floral room, which Antoinetta announced was called the Sunshine Room. There were novels, an easel, several floral sofas, and vases of fresh spring blossoms throughout. The plush rugs were comfortable under Mary's feet as she was pulled along by her new friend, and the windows stood at least nine feet tall.

"This is my favorite room," Antoinetta confessed.

Then the heiress tugged our Mary Potts into a different space—a portrait-laden oak and velvet dining room just as big as The Drabbe's, but infinitely nicer, with long, dark tables. There, they ran up a simple back staircase and walked down what Antoinetta called the guest hallway in her rushed verbal tour, as it was where all six guest rooms were located. Mary was able to peek inside one and spied a large, four-poster bed, complete with a desk, floral sofa, plush carpets, and a private fireplace.

It was almost too much luxury to take in. She'd never even known such nice things existed, and she wondered how she had been so lucky to experience more than the average guest—a personal tour from the heiress herself.

Then the two stopped at the top of the grand staircase, as the clock struck seven.

"We must make a grand entrance." Antoinetta adjusted her hat and smoothed flyaway hairs back into her low-lying bun. Sensing Mary's trepidation, she said, "As heiress and hostess, I insist on it."

What could our lie-trapped Mary Potts say now? Her own words from her self-counsel only minutes before rang in her head: *You mustn't draw attention to yourself, or entertain too much...*

Antoinetta took her arm and the two gracefully walked down each carpeted step. Antoinetta held her head slightly upward to allow for admiration, but Mary's eyes drifted to the foot of the staircase where so many handsome and well-built gentlemen and a great number of probable nobility stood in awe of the pair, some smiling, some giving small applause. She could scarcely believe that the attention of so many of the male sex was on herself. Roy and Briddie were right; this *was* a dream.

As she kept descending step by step, relishing the attention from so many fine men, attention for which she had longed for over a decade, all her personal vows for the evening instantly evaporated like steam from a hot drink. Because there, among the gentry and nobles, was a face she could never forget. It was the gentleman, Mr. Singh, who had encouraged her and kissed her hand. Mr. Singh, with whom she had shared a forbidden and secret touch that tingled her straight to her soul.

She was even more exhilarated to see that his eyes were on her. She wanted to play it cool and look away, but she couldn't. They were watching each other, and suddenly, he smiled and gave her a slight nod.

Where was her control now? And her acting skills? She didn't want to smile, but even so, she was grinning from ear to ear. That is, until she noticed he was standing right next to Arthur Prickwhile, whose eyes she also met, just briefly. She remembered his secret caress of her stocking. Now, she shared two intimate secrets with two different gentlemen, and they appeared to be friends.

Indeed, as Mary reached the bottom of the staircase, she picked up on their conversation. Briddie had told her that many times a man will make himself heard, though he acts like he is speaking in confidence. It is to say, his intention is to be overheard. This is the sensation that Mary encountered as she heard Mr. Singh's warm voice poetically say, "Wine and grapes." He was referring to the rich color of their dresses, crimson and violet, and it seemed to her very clever and nice.

"Blood and bruises, if you ask me," Arthur quipped, evoking chuckles from his mates.

"What is her name?" Singh asked now, a bit louder.

"She's Mary Riboneaux, from Greece, and I'll have her for my own. Who is to say, I might even marry her." At this, Arthur's friends erupted in laughter and Mary blushed. "And she shows no interest in me, which makes the chase even more exciting."

Antoinetta led Mary into the ballroom, away from the stairs, and with such chatter and noise therein, she was unable to overhear any more of what Mr. Singh and Arthur were saying, though it was clear the two men wanted to be heard.

Could it be that two men were already vying for her attention, and one that she practically already loved? Luckily, Mary was not easily overwhelmed, or she might faint, as she knew fancier women of the time would do when becoming emotional. And she didn't think it would be too hard to muster up a fainting spell—Myrtle had pulled the corset strings with her whole body's fortitude tonight.

The ballroom itself was a masterpiece, featuring frescoed ceilings, fine polished floors, buffet tables, and plush seating along the walls, of course. Everyone came to dance more than lounge. And dance they did, after Antoinetta spoke some brief words of gratitude to the crowd and offered a champagne toast.

Mary was very popular with all the people Antoinetta introduced her to, though she stayed on the right end of the ballroom, since Lady Huntron was seated on the far left. Guests approached the elder woman and greeted her continually. This was both good and bad. Lady Huntron would probably not remember if Mary had greeted her or not if she became brave enough to present herself to the lady, which was an advantage. The drawback, of course, was that Antoinetta or others may expect or even urge Mary to greet her.

It was not long until Antoinetta was asked to dance by a friend of her late father's. She apologetically took her leave, but Mary told her not to worry. And it was perfect timing, because at that moment, as she sipped her punch, she saw Mr. Singh and his gorgeous, dark features as he made his way through the crowd, darting his eyes all about, obviously in search of something... or some*one*.

He saw her, then in no time, he reached her.

"Mary," he breathed out as his mouth broke into a smile.

"Mr. Singh," Mary said and smiled back. If he saw her here, dressed like this, perhaps he could accept that she was a pub girl. After all, he had been poor, too. Surely, he wouldn't hold it against her. Perhaps they could talk about their touch in the courtyard of The Drabbe. Perhaps they could have a future and—

"How... do you know my name?" he asked, cocking his head.

Suddenly, Mary's heart fell.

The soot. The dark. The barmaid's cap.

Mr. Singh didn't even recognize her. He was here, like all the other fine gentlemen, in order to procure an advantageous match and mingle with people of his own class—not barmaids. Poor he was no longer. The way he was dressed tonight, he looked to be the richest in the room. Friend of the heir, Singh. International traveler, Singh.

Mary had to hide her disappointment, and her true identity. He could never know that the soot girl was her.

"I—I—" Mary stammered. Then she spotted Arthur. "I rode here with the Prickwhiles. Arthur told me about you."

"Oh, yes, dear Arthur. I'm staying here at Mannerley as his guest. Where are you lodging?"

"An apartment," Mary lied.

"In town?"

Mary smiled and sighed. She just couldn't give him too much information, so she decided to change the subject and enjoy what time she could with him. "Mr. Singh, do you like to dance?"

"Shouldn't the man ask the woman to dance?" he mused.

"Indeed, *shouldn't* you?" Mary asked mischievously. Singh reared back and laughed.

"Now, I know why Arthur is captivated with you," he said, then took her gloved hand and led her onto the ballroom floor. There, he proceeded to twirl her around like the floor was oiled.

She had danced many times with her friends and family at The Drabbe, and Roy himself was not a bad dancer. He loved teaching his sister-in-law, wife, and children the popular moves. Every holiday was celebrated with a dance. But never had she ever been swung around quite like this. Mr. Singh was a master at this art.

Mary never, ever wanted this moment to end. She longed to remove her gloves and grasp his hand like she did in the dark courtyard three days before, to see if the mysterious energy would course through them as it had then.

They danced and swayed and moved in time with the orchestra, and as they danced, the distance between their faces reduced and reduced, until they were looking into each other's eyes comfortably; no longer were they strangers who kept each other safely away. Mary sensed she had come to know him intimately. This was it; this was Mary's dream.

"May I?"

Mr. Singh and Mary stopped their dance at the very moment Arthur posed his question. Mary tried to hide her disappointment. She never wanted to leave Mr. Singh, never in a million years.

Mr. Singh looked at Mary and then back at Arthur. Quickly, he released her waist and her hand, holding his hands briefly in the air as if caught, or as if she were burning hot to the touch. "Of course," he muttered, smiled politely, and then bowed and walked away.

Arthur placed his hands where Singh's had been, and Mary fell into step under his lead, though without speaking at first. She needed all her mental energy to seem docile and controlled and confident on the outside, though with every loop or turn, she surveyed the room for her darling Mr. Singh.

Arthur's dancing was rougher, heavier than Singh's feathery touch. And Mary did not dislike it, or him. He was altogether handsome, taller than Singh, bigger than Singh, very much more British than Singh. But he certainly wasn't as open; he held something back, perhaps mirroring her own cloistering of facts. She got the feeling from Arthur that he was not completely benevolent.

Arthur finally broke the silence.

"You are preoccupied, Mary Agnes."

It was apparent that Antoinetta had informed Arthur of the added *Agnes* at some point, along with everyone else at the ball as well, including, most probably, Mr. Singh. Mary couldn't decide if this was good or bad, but thinking of Antoinetta at that moment gave Mary the perfect excuse for the distracted look she evidently wore.

"Yes, sir. I am looking for your sister," she said, dodging his gaze.

"She is with Lady Huntron, as she should be."

"Won't she be asked to dance again?" Mary asked.

"Certainly. She'll dance with most of these gentlemen. Her beau, Walt Corning, is here. He's a nice lad. A bit boring." Arthur smirked briefly after judging Walt. "He doesn't dance."

"I have heard he is to be a solicitor," Mary mentioned politely, referring to Walt's study of the law. "It is a perfectly suitable profession for a gentleman."

"Hmm," Arthur affirmed. "And how do you feel about businessmen heirs?"

"The question is specific," Mary said, fighting against a small laugh which his inquiry evoked. "But I shall answer it with generalities. I believe the way of the future will not be lords and lands, but rather power through education; a hierarchical elitism of earned titles, if you will. So that anyone may be anything." If she were truly bold, she would add that any *woman* may be anything as well.

"You have strong, intelligent opinions, Mary Agnes," Arthur said, admiration in his eyes. "I must twirl you in recompense." He did, and again, her smile broke through.

At that time, the music and dance changed, and Mary was suddenly held in Arthur's rhythmic embrace a bit closer than she would have liked. Indeed, their chests brushed, and his mouth was near her ear. After dancing a while, he remarked, "So it must be that you have not yet greeted Lady Huntron."

Now, Mary's stomach was truly in knots, as she feared the old woman would not recognize her and throw her out, or worse, that the real Agnes was also at the party. She had no reason to give Arthur for not greeting the woman, and could not come up with one, so she quickly prayed and wondered if it was such a sin to ask God to help with a lie.

And her method of avoiding Lady Huntron was very much sinful, as she opted for pulling Arthur closer to herself, so her chest pressed firmly against his, and then she whispered in his ear which stood a bit taller than her mouth that she was having too much of a grand time to stop and greet the old woman. "Besides," she said, taking a risk, "she won't remember me very well. I was little when she knew me, and her memory is bad."

"Say no more," he said, passion in his voice, holding her close.

She knew she had awoken pleasure in him of the type that gentlemen try to restrain. Free reign to such things, and so quickly, could bring no good.

"You couldn't pay me to let you go anywhere right now the way you're holding onto me."

And you mustn't fall in love or cause some bloke to love you.

Mary closed her eyes against this pang of guilt. How had her planned incognito evening already become so complicated?

When she opened her eyes again, Arthur was twirling her, and she caught sight of Mr. Singh. The look on his face was pure jealousy and disappointment. Though he was far from her, he turned dejectedly and exited the dance. Mary was very happy when, moments later, Antoinetta rescued her from the sensual embrace and invited her to take a walk in the gardens for some conversation, and because, she disclosed to Mary, it was not entirely appropriate that Mary and Arthur dance so very closely.

At around three in the morning, Mary had long since been back in the ballroom dancing the night away with as many handsome men as she could, just for the fun of it, and Antoinetta had occupied her brother with many single friends to protect Mary. Singh was nowhere to be found.

The guests said their goodbyes little by little, and Antoinetta came up to Mary, smiling that sweet smile. Her hat was long gone, and her bun flopped down flaccidly, but the messiness was becoming to her face. She introduced her beau, Walt Corning, a plain fellow with dark hair that was plastered flat around his pale, pudgy face. He seemed deeply shy, or at least very quiet. And then Antoinetta got into business as her brother Arthur approached to join them in the emptying ballroom.

"Lady Huntron has just gone off to bed. Is it true you never greeted her tonight, Mary Agnes?" Antoinetta asked, concerned, and Mary confirmed. "That cannot be so, my dear. I must teach you the politeness of English customs. Shame on you." She clicked her tongue. "At any rate, I've pressed her to allow you to stay the week with us here at Mannerley. We have another two here with us from India— Oh, you'll love my dear Mrs. Singh. She is not at the party tonight because she does not enjoy them, but she is a true and warm spirit. Won't you stay? Lady Huntron's already sent to prepare a guest room."

Mrs. Singh? Surely it could not be so. Mr. Singh wouldn't betray a wife; he was too much of a gentleman.

But he did leave the dance early, and never returned.

He had kissed her hand, privately, in the courtyard of The Drabbe, thinking she was a different, working-class woman than the fancily dressed girl before him tonight.

Could Mr. Singh be a womanizer? Arthur seemed more like one, just from initial impressions. She was so very confused. But it seemed there was indeed a *Mrs.* Singh.

Mary couldn't help but feel hoodwinked, and even a bit angry at being tricked. No, she wouldn't stay, if only because of this. Besides, she had no belongings with her, and Roy was waiting to take her back to The Drabbe in his carriage parked behind the jewelry shop. The party was over; it was time for her to disappear from these people's lives. She had lived and dreamed enough for a lifetime, and had come to find that being one of the higher class was more complicated than it seemed.

"Oh no, I couldn't impose," Mary said, naming her excuse. "I don't even have other clothing with me."

"Nonsense, what will you need? I imagine since you were walking earlier, you had arrangements at an apartment in Mannerley Town? I will lend you a fresh chemise for sleeping and you can have your things sent tomorrow."

"Yes, you can sleep in the chemise," Arthur suggested softly, brushing away a black curl which clung to Mary's neck with sweat, and she could tell he was imagining what that might look like. "But if you fully deny our invitation, I shall have to escort you to your apartment. A girl of society walking alone at night is not to be borne."

"Then I accept," Mary blurted impulsively because she had no apartment to go to. She smiled and the group mirrored her expression and nodded at one another with Antoinetta and Walt promptly taking their leave.

Inside, Mary was very anxious and took a moment to finish her punch and sort out her thoughts while Arthur saw off the last few guests. Roy would know, come first light, that she had been held up. She hoped he would wait for her, and that somehow, she could make an apt escape, vanishing as if she had never existed. Indeed, Mary Agnes Riboneaux did not exist.

"Shall we?" Arthur Prickwhile offered her his arm and together they slowly walked up to the guest hall, which was quiet and dim. Mary opened the door and spied the clean chemise laid out on the bed. Then it became apparent that Arthur was intent on inviting himself inside.

"I've had a very grand time tonight," Mary said, stepping inside quickly and letting the door come between herself and Arthur, though she left a small space for talking.

He laughed and sighed at the same time. "So you are, after all, a *little* bit Victorian, then?"

"Yes," Mary admitted and blushed.

"So, the fun must end. I see. Good night to you." Arthur took his leave. She watched him walk down the guest hall to his own room, two doors from hers. His gait was attractive; his presence imposing. There was something hidden in him that she wanted to believe was sinister, but she had so little experience with men that she could not know if it was only the lustful passion that she had awoken in him by necessity, poor fellow, or something worse. As she watched him, it occurred to her that if she could not have Mr. Singh, then Arthur would not be a terrible alternative.

She bid the thought away with a few rapid blinks. It was not right. Tomorrow, she would leave behind all these people and all the confusion and all the attraction.

Servants were approaching, and she realized that it was odd to be staring at him as he walked off.

She closed her door.

Declan Thobbs made his way up the stairway at Mannerley and across the guest hall after an intense night at his new job. He hated all the fancy people who spent more than his life earnings on attire for such a silly, pompous affair as a springtime ball. It was unfair to be expected to know everything on his second night of work. This was especially the case, because on his first night at Mannerley, instead of receiving training, the old lunatic Huntron had made him sit for a routine employee photograph to be hung in the servants' quarters among scores of others, as if it were some great honor.

Oh, how he loathed his life and longed for a different situation.

He saw a rich young dandy, the heir himself, Arthur Prickwhile standing by a young woman's door, and of course he knew what he was up to. Declan took joy when Arthur's advances were rejected, and he went walking across to his own room. Declan passed by and glanced in just as the young woman shut her door, and saw a familiar tanned face and long black ringlets, and eyelashes like dove's wings.

He was positive he knew her, but could not for the life of him remember how.

CHAPTER FIVE

The Second Day—Morning

Somehow Mary Potts slept, and slept hard, despite her nervousness over Roy. The linens and mattress of the guestroom bed must have enveloped her in a silky warmth her tired body couldn't resist. She awoke, jolting up to see the cuckoo clock, and gasping that it was half past eleven. Eschewing fashion, she threw on her dress from the night before without the corset. Though, she did not really need a corset, as she had a naturally small waist.

In the wardrobe, she was happy to see her—or Agnes's—velvet jacket, which she promptly put on. There was also a small, printed image of Mannerley in full bloom. Antoinetta had promised her a better souvenir, after all, and this was it. On the back was written in pencil: *With Love, Ant.* She must have arranged for both things to be put in the guest room when it was ordered by Lady Huntron.

Mary was quite sad about having to lose Antoinetta; it had been nice to have a real friend. But leave she must, so she bolted out her room and down the stairs, trying to be as quiet as she could, with a plan to run out the front door in the direction of poor, worried Roy as quickly as possible.

"There you are!" Antoinetta exclaimed from the Sunshine Room which was in direct view of the front entryway. "Come and join us."

"I-I was going for a walk," Mary protested nervously, but Antoinetta was already making her way to Mary and taking her arm. She gave her another speech as they walked toward the floral sofas of the Sunshine Room. Mary realized that her new friend was very fond of chatting while in motion.

"Don't be silly, Mary Agnes. We're having a cold luncheon, well, cakes and scones and such. And after last night, we all need the fresh air as much as you do. We shall all take a walk after eating, then have a rest, for Lady Blanche Huntron has invited us six to dine with her tonight instead of at a separate hour. She is very much looking forward to seeing you; she loves young and pretty faces."

Mary could not protest. What excuse could she have? Certainly, anything she came up with would just add to her precariously teetering tower of lies.

When the two young women stepped on the plush, oriental carpets of the Sunshine Room, the men arose. There was Arthur Prickwhile looking as devilishly handsome as ever, but his face seemed to show that he had suffered all night by Mary's fault. His look seemed to soften when he saw her, and he smiled a bit. Next to him was Walt Corning who had all the emotion and intrigue of a leftover dinner roll. Across from them was Mr. Singh.

Upon seeing him her heart fluttered. From her place on Antoinetta's arm, she smiled a tight smile. But she wanted to run to him and embrace him. Try as she might, she couldn't quell the truth rising inside her. She was crazy about him. Skin like tea with a splash of milk in it, black silky hair, strong black brow, and rosy, plump lips. He was altogether handsome and seemed to be well-rested. He was the next to speak, and graciously.

"Mary Agnes, a pleasure to see you again. I must say, it was wonderful to dance with you last night. You are an excellent dancer."

"Likewise," Mary managed and curtsied.

"Allow me," Arthur interrupted briskly, seemingly unable to endure any amiable contact between Mr. Singh and Mary. "Mary, you already know Mr. Walt Corning and Mr. Advik Singh. This is Mrs. Indira Singh." He motioned toward a small woman in a petal-pink saree who sat at Mr. Singh's side, then back to Mary. "Miss Mary Agnes Riboneaux."

Mary curtsied nervously, her heart picking up speed beneath her violet bodice.

So, it was true. She was crushed all over again, and she revisited her feelings of being duped and her rising anger from the previous night. The woman beside the captivating Mr. Singh was small and intense, with eyes that burned through Mary as if she knew all about her.

His wife. She curtsied as well, though minimally.

And she did not smile.

"Mrs. Singh, what a pleasure. Mr. Singh is wholly charming on the ballroom floor. You must be very proud," Mary said forcedly, hoping to ingratiate herself with the lady. She seemed older than Mr. Singh, thirty or more, and her hair was the thickest, softest shade of black. It cascaded from her head lusciously. Mary could not tell if her intense eyes were lined with paint, or if her lashes were just so thick as to make them stand out so boldly. She was pretty; very pretty. *Too* pretty. And she said nothing to Mary's attempt at conversation, so Mary tried again. "I did not have the pleasure of meeting you last night. That is a shame."

"I don't attend parties," Mrs. Singh said dryly in perfect English. Mary looked for something to say, and found nothing. She clenched her fists at her sides, intimidated. Her fingers stuck to her clammy palms.

"Have a seat by me," Arthur said.

Mary was thankful he broke the silence, but regretted that he seemed to be claiming her for himself so early in the day. She sat, as did Antoinetta and the men, and her thoughts raced about her lies, the night before, Mrs. Singh, Agnes, and Roy. She needed a quiet room away from them all to sort it out, upset and overwhelmed as she was. Mrs. Indira Singh's cold behavior had seemingly pushed her over the emotional edge on which she had teetered all night. The edge between excitement and anxiety.

A young man's freckled arm served her tea, but she did not look up at his face consumed as she was in her thoughts. "Thank you," Mary mumbled absently.

"Do you make it a habit of thanking your servants in Greece?" Arthur asked, and his sister rolled her sweet blue eyes and scoffed dramatically, while Mr. Singh laughed at his friend in scandalized disbelief. "What? It's only a question! And a valid one."

I am the servant, Mary wanted to say, but instead she said, "Actually, yes."

Antoinetta swirled her tea in her teacup, made of fine cream-colored china, and embellished with little golden roses. "Well then, they must be very happy servants. You all know Lady Huntron always makes it a point to thank her workers and give them little gifts. I dare say most of the people working here are quite content to do so. Despite her antics and her moments of confusion, she is a kind woman who loves justice, and tries to do right by all," Antoinetta said.

"Remind me," Mrs. Indira Singh said, dark eyes burning through Arthur, "how exactly you came to be the heir of this place? You are not a Huntron, and Lady Blanche is not your mother."

"My father was her nephew, and she adored him. She never had children. So, we are the closest relatives she has."

"We? You mean, both you and Antoinetta will inherit the property together? How will that be managed?" Indira pressed.

"It's simple, really. We'll both be the owners, with the overseeing help of a trustee."

"Unless, of course," Indira said quietly, raising her teacup slowly to her mouth, "one of you were to die."

Silence settled around them, and Arthur and Advik shot each other a startled look. The quiet went on for far too long, and Mary was unsure why such a comment was weighing so heavily on the group. Only Walt seemed unaware of the change of feeling, licking his fingers after eating a buttery pastry. Mary was completely lost.

"Oh, come now," Indira said, this time much more gaily. "It was only a joke."

Everyone relaxed, exhaled, and smiled out their stress, with Arthur chuckling relievedly and dabbing at his brow with a wine-colored cloth napkin, before glancing out the window.

"Don't you think it odd that we haven't seen Lady Huntron this morning at all? She is usually taking her stroll around the gardens by now," Arthur said with a puzzled look on his face as if suddenly remembering.

"I sense the liveliness of last night must have worn her down. She must be in her chambers in the west wing, sleeping." This spoke Indira in a tone smooth and calm as butter, a very different tone than the one she used toward Mary.

"Well, if you say it, my dear Mrs. Singh, it must be so," Antoinetta remarked, smiling at her friend, then said to Mary in particular, "Indira is said to have a sixth sense in many matters of the heart and soul."

Or it could have just been a lucky guess, since the woman is eighty-three and partied all night, thought Mary. Now, she understood the upset at Indira's comment about death. These fancy people really took Indira's predictions and interpretations seriously.

"Is that so?" Mary ended up saying, smiling with squinting eyes at Mrs. Indira Singh, who glared back, face wiped clean of emotion.

"Hmm," affirmed Arthur while sipping his tea. He took a scone in his hand and went on, "And Mr. Advik Singh has no extra senses—no sense *at all*, really—but he's practically a doctor, having been taken in and raised by one from boyhood. He can suggest healing medicines and treatments for a variety of ailments. In India, he is of the Kshatriya caste." Arthur said this last part as if it meant something to Mary; as if she would understand.

"A man of skill in medicine will never be without work, friends, or money," Mary said safely, to which her new friends agreed heartily and outwardly, except for Mrs. Singh of course, who only picked at some cake.

"Actually, my friend speaks a bit naively. My doctoring abilities have nothing to do with me being kshatriya. The kshatriya are military people; they fight with bravery when needed, and govern with peace when possible," Mr. Singh explained.

"What I meant to point out is that you are part of the upper caste in India, not the lower, just as a medical doctor is someone very well-respected here," Arthur said.

"Ah, but if I am so naturally important as you say, then why did I have to be rescued by an Englishman who found me picking through a rubbish heap for something to sell? Poor is poor." Mr. Singh was only playfully frustrated with his friend. He put Arthur in his place, but with a smile, gentleness, and patience.

Mary smoothed the dress over her thighs. She remembered picking through garbage well. She had done it daily for over a decade. The dress she now wore was a rubbish-pile-find. Why, though she was angry at him, did she find herself even more endeared to Mr. Singh?

"Well, I should venture to say that you were rescued because you are kshatriya. I think if you were any lower caste the man would have left you there."

"Perhaps, my friend, perhaps," Mr. Singh acquiesced, "but let us just be glad that the castes do not exist in England. Here is a land where anyone can be anything, and there is no organization based on class. I find the whole system abhorrent and unfair. You English are lucky to be free from it."

Mary did not know whether to laugh out loud at such absurdity or run out the door and never come back, but before she could stop it, her tongue was at work, riding into Mr. Singh and releasing some of her pent-up tension toward him.

"Sir, I'll have you know that the lower classes in England are the working poor, and life for them is quite stuck. They can have no dreams other than penny pinching, or perhaps crime, which seems to bring a shilling quicker than labor. They are categorized by what they can afford to wear, the accent they absorb from youth, and their station in life, it is to say, their profession or title or relations. And most certainly it is based on one's inheritances and income."

To Mary's surprise, Antoinetta chimed in next. "And what of women, Mr. Singh? We are wholly second-class in England. Expected to stay indoors with no say in anything. Why, I can't even travel alone. Meanwhile, my brother can go and come as he pleases."

"Antoinetta, thank you!" Mary breathed out, grateful and shocked. Antoinetta was a purehearted woman, no doubt, and it was not difficult to become her instant friend. Mary turned back to Mr. Singh. "So, imagine the poor person I described, but also make that person a female—a hard life, indeed."

"I have not seen this part of England," Mr. Singh said kindly but defensively. "And I would dare to say that you could take the poorest working girl in England with the fewest prospects and dreams, dress her up nicely, fix her hair, and she may even have soireed with us last night at the ball, unperceived. This, Miss Riboneaux, could *never* happen in India."

"It is true, we are not a hateful or prejudiced society... anymore," Walt Corning said dully, eating a scone, crumbs dangling from his thin lips.

Mr. Singh stirred and drank his breakfast tea as if nothing at all had happened in this brief exchange, but Mary's heart pounded hard, and her face grew hot. Could Mr. Singh know her secret after all? One quick glance at his aloof visage put her at ease; he most certainly did *not* know he had just described her. He'd spoken hypothetically, not cryptically.

Mary suddenly took courage now that she was mostly sure Mr. Singh didn't suspect anything. "Ah, but where would this poor girl get the dress that costs months of her pay? And how would she enter an invitation-only party?" Mary's face grew even hotter from anger. These people knew nothing of her struggles but assumed they knew it all, and worse still, did not care to see the truth. To them—except to perceptive Antoinetta—there was no struggle in England because they did not suffer it, and to them this idea was not open for debate.

"Perhaps, fate?" Indira smirked at Mary. "Those who would escape their class must have the help of God and destiny. And why, might I ask, do you take personal offense at these fellows' suppositions of class and suffering?"

Mary did not answer because she perceived Indira already knew.

Advik Singh tilted his head at Indira then Mary, intrigued with the conversation, but then changed the subject. "Prickwhile, your lady friend here, Mary Agnes, is it? Have you thought she could pass for Indian, except for the curls?"

"Mr. Singh, many Indian ladies have curls," Arthur scoffed.

"Do they? I've never noticed. But you, of course, are the expert observer of the female sex. For this Mary Agnes creature, all we'd need is a bindi right..." Mr. Singh leaned over the small tea table they were crowded around and placed his thumb on her forehead. "Here."

A shock coursed through her entire body, and she shivered.

He must have experienced the energy, too, because he twitched and quickly said, "I'm sorry," removing his hand and leaning back to his place.

"No, it's quite alright," she said, eyes wide, and forgot for a moment that there were others with them, and completely forgot her anger and heartbreak. Mary could not understand what it was about this enchanting Mr. Singh that quite literally electrified her body. This married, captivating Mr. Singh who had gently touched her head. This Mr. Singh who danced like velvet.

"Well, shall we all go for a walk then?" Antoinetta offered now that everyone had finished their cold meal, and the people arose. "Ah, Mary Agnes, let me lend you a dress. Yours is much too formal, and you're about my size."

After Mary had fetched the dress from Antoinetta—a lightweight, floral thing—a lady's maid helped Mary put it on and she hurried down the steps toward the rest of the group, whom she assumed to be outside. But, as she rounded the corner of the entryway, she stopped and shrunk back, seeing Mrs. Indira Singh talking to Mr. Advik Singh candidly about Mary as they strolled along the front walk.

"I do not know exactly what it is, but I will find out. There is something strangely deceitful in Mary Agnes's energy. Do beware of her," she warned him.

And our poor Mary Potts, who never intended to hurt anyone, and just wanted to be done with this whole charade, became even more nervous and upset.

CHAPTER SIX
The Second Day—Afternoon

Finally, after almost an hour out of doors, first on Antoinetta's arm listening to her stories, then on Arthur's arm who was quiet from tiredness, he said, and even once on Walt's chubby arm to learn of pond grasses, of which he knew too much—finally, finally Mary had her chance to sprint to Roy. The three fellows had trotted off together to inspect some game traps and talk of sport. Antoinetta and Indira were absorbed in a conversation about romance and their respective partners.

Antoinetta had motioned for Mary to run up with them, but Mary came up with the excuse that she was enjoying the quiet and cool air alone, as she had a bit of a headache from the drinks and dancing the night before. To her surprise, they did not press her. Mrs. Singh even seemed relieved that Mary would not join them. So, as the male group advanced and veered right, and the two ladies went on toward the left absorbed in their intimate tales, Mary fell further and further and further back until they were all out of earshot, at which time she turned sharply and ran for her ever-loving life in the opposite direction toward the entryway of the estate.

The front drive was long, and now, she gathered Antoinetta's floral day dress into her arms and positively leapt over last night's manure piles and toward the front gate, where she had to explain to the gatekeeper that she had arranged to retrieve her trunk from her apartment, if he would just let her out. He did, but entirely too slowly, and she feared it would give time for the others to miss her and seek her out.

Once she was freed, she bolted across the town walk and through an alleyway and behind the jewelry shop where she startled Roy who jumped down from his box seat, blond hair fluffed up from a bad resting position. She wanted to run into his arms and hug him and kiss his face and be consoled for all her nervousness.

"Not now, child, don't fall on me here. They'll see." Roy held her back.

"Let's go, let's leave. Start the horses!" Mary looked over her shoulder quickly.

"No, Mary. No," Roy said, and then struggled with the heavy trunk in the back of the buggy, bringing it out and setting it before her.

"How did you—?" Mary was beyond confused. She had last seen the trunk at The Drabbe, where she left it after getting dressed for the ball. The Drabbe seemed a universe away after all she had experienced.

"Oh, at about three o'clock this morning when I was waking up and preparing to start off to find you, I heard much talk from happy guests retreating to their rooms and apartments. Talk of an enchanting new friend, one Mary Riboneaux, with long black curls, who danced so well and was so kind, and who had been *invited to stay the week with the heir and heiress Prickwhile at Mannerley.*" He spoke these last fifteen words or so in escalated excitement, each word topping the one before, until he was left smiling and gasping with pride.

"So naturally, I left immediately for The Drabbe, got there in two hours flat, loaded the trunk and another of your casual day dresses that you wear on your off days, as well as your own leather boots, and headed straight back here to the spot where I left you last night."

She could scarcely believe it all and rubbed her brow in bewilderment. "Oh, Roy. I've been so dreadfully nervous. I feared for you out here worried for me. I had no way to come before now, believe me." Mary's eyes filled with tears for Roy's sacrifice and great effort all for her sake.

"Mary, what? I'm fine!" He laughed sincerely at her fears. "Don't worry, my child. I'm made for this. A life of service, it's in my heart. And there's no one I'd rather serve than a lady fine as you, that I raised meself." Now, her tears fell, and she wanted to hug him again. They only held each other at the elbows, and she gave him a quick and airy kiss on his stubbly cheek. Her sweet and sacrificial Roy.

"There you are," Arthur Prickwhile said, surprising Mary and Roy both, who separated instantly and looked at him with wide eyes, as if caught in a crime. "The Drabbe... where's that?" Arthur asked after reading the buggy, slipping Roy a few too many coins as a gracious tip, and picking up the suitcase. Roy marveled at the sum in his hands. Arthur grunted. "Heavens, it's heavy." His brow broke to a sweat, but he still looked dashing, perhaps even manlier than before.

"It's a ways off. They sent this buggy to bring my things." Mary was nervous the explanations wouldn't hold up and she would be exposed.

On the contrary, Arthur couldn't have cared less about the matter, and never even properly looked at Roy. "Mm hmm, yes, darling. Singh! Singh, come help me with this trunk."

It was then Mary realized that Mr. and Mrs. Singh were now by the window of the jewelry shop just a stone's throw away, and perhaps within earshot. How long had they been there? Mary swallowed hard.

Advik Singh jogged up athletically and the two took the trunk. "Indira, accompany Miss Riboneaux," Advik instructed, and the two men walked ahead toward Mannerley's gate hauling the awkward luggage between them.

Mary took Indira's tiny arm, brown skin smooth as satin, and not a hair on it. She glanced back and secretly winked at Roy, who had put on his hat, and he tilted his brim her way before mounting himself in the box seat.

"Mary Agnes, it is my perception that you were speaking with great intimacy with the buggy driver," Mrs. Singh remarked as they made a good pace up the front drive.

Then she said no more, and Mary realized it was her turn to speak. "Yes," Mary said, not able to scrape up any excuse. They were silent until they reached the staircase in the entryway. Mary burst with awkward tension, fearing Indira knew everything. In contrast, Mrs. Indira Singh seemed to glide calmly both physically and socially, not in the least perturbed.

"Forgive me, I must unpack," Mary said, taking her leave, loosening her arm, and running up the stairs. When she got to the top, she heard Indira speak again, and stopped to look at her standing among shadows at the bottom of the staircase, a specter in pink. Mary's chest heaved with anxious breaths.

"And I observe that you are fond of running. Now on the stairs, but earlier, I saw you almost take flight down the front drive toward the gate. It was I who called the gentlemen to help. It seemed as if you were apt to run away forever. I wonder what could be so bad that you must attempt an escape. Perhaps a temptation in the form of the male sex?"

"N-No," Mary stuttered, "not at all." They looked at one another for just a moment more. Then Mary wished her a good afternoon and went to her chamber. There were Arthur and Advik waiting for her to open the door, which she did. They set the trunk on the plush rug in front of the fireplace.

"Oh, what a relief," Mary fibbed. It was far from a relief to still be in possession of Agnes's things—to still have to find a way to keep up with all her lies. "Thank you both."

"Mary Agnes, you look... frightened," Mr. Singh said, a look of pure compassion on his chiseled face. "Are you quite alright?"

"Oh, yes." She looked down and laughed. "It's nothing more than tiredness. The party... and the walk."

"Shall I fetch you some herbal tea, or something small to eat, before you rest?" This said Arthur, moving close and placing his index finger under her chin to lift her face to his. Her eyes darted to Mr. Singh. He had turned away at this display of affection and did not look content. No, he looked very much annoyed, hands in pockets and lips pursed.

"Yes," Mary heard herself say. "Yes, please. That would be very kind of you."

"Perhaps," Mr. Singh suggested, "we should ask a server to bring the herbal infusion. It shouldn't be right for a man of your status, Arthur, to dally about sporting trays and serving guests."

"Oh, I don't mind with a girl like Mary Agnes." Arthur peered into Mary's eyes, biting his bottom lip.

It wasn't that she disliked him, and he did stir passions greatly within her. She relished the attention he bestowed on her. Just to be the object of his obsession was like a dream. The problem with Arthur was that she did not *understand* him, and she feared a hidden malevolence within him. He was risky and unreadable.

But at least he wasn't married.

"Well then, allow me to say what I truly think," Mr. Singh continued gently, "which is that I am going to retire to my chamber to rest before dinner with Lady Huntron as we all should, tired as we are, and it is not appropriate for you to deliver the herbal tea and food to Mary's room because that would put you here with her, alone, which should not be done."

Would Advik now tell Arthur and Mary what should not be done and give them a lesson on morality? Mary fought against a loud scoff.

"Yes." Arthur dropped his hand from Mary's chin and stepped toward his friend. "Yes, you have spoken correctly. It should not be done. It would not look entirely right, though I am harmless. I will order the tea to be brought to her. Good afternoon to you, Mary." And the two dapper gentlemen left her presence, the essence of their fresh colognes trailing behind them.

Now, our Mary Potts offset her nerves by organizing Agnes's clothes, which she had almost forgotten were Agnes's, and that Agnes existed and was somewhere alive and possibly lamenting her situation or seeking this same suitcase. It must be said that the thought of Lady Huntron finding out her lie was intimidating to her, but Mary resolved to answer all questions vaguely at dinner, or better yet, lead Lady Huntron to answer her own questions. Yes, that was the ticket. She laughed by herself at her own cleverness, and then she heard the door of her room shut sharply. She did an about-face to see Declan Thobbs in full Mannerley service uniform, holding her infusion tray and plastered with an evil grin.

"Well, Mary Potts. Or should I say Mary Ribbon-O? Or should I say Agnes? Ha!" He set the tray down and moved close. Mary became faint and sat on the edge of her bed. She did not fear he would harm her intimately, for Declan did not have it in him. But she knew his sinister glare and smile meant she would soon be faced with much trouble.

"I saw you last night, then again this morning in the Sunshine Room. When they called you Mary Agnes, it hit me—Mary! Of course, Mary Potts, sister of the people who threw me onto the street for no reason. The people who tried to ruin my life. I barely recognized you with your barmaid cap gone and with the soot scrubbed from your nails. Oh, I know your secret well. Somehow you have obtained these fine clothes and here you are trying to trick a wealthy man into marrying you."

"No, no, I'm not—"

"And you have your pick of them!" interrupted Declan. "They're falling all over you, Mary Potts. If only they knew who you really were. Do you think they'd be interested? They wouldn't even look at the likes of you. And they will know who you really are by week's end unless you pay me well."

"Declan, please. Allow me to explain," Mary pleaded, speaking low. "I only intended to come to the ball just to see what it was like, but now I'm trapped here all week because they've loved me so much. The suitcase was found, not stolen, or bought. I'm still poor. I can't pay you anything. I have nothing." Mary's bewildered eyes implored him for compassion. His green ones seemed resolved to continue the manipulation and never softened, not once.

"I figured as much. So, I'll name the price of my silence: Arthur Prickwhile's antique gold pocket watch will suffice. I have a black-market connection in Port Lazáre who is desperate to have it, and will offer a good sum. You know I scoped out the valuables when I started this employment and informed him. One day I'll sell something so fine I will never have to work again." Declan's smile faded and the hollowness of his eyes behind his clammy white skin was all too evident as he gazed off, overcome by his sordid fantasy.

"You poor, lost soul," Mary said, now tearful.

"The watch. Or I tell." Declan started to leave, then turned back, took one of Mary's biscuits, stuffed it in his mouth, and walked out the door.

Mary shut the door behind him and turned her key in the lock. And then she ran and crashed on her bed, shaking under deep sobs. No one here knew her, and the only one who did would use the knowledge against her. A handsome but possibly evil man loved her, but her heart wanted what she couldn't have. Absolutely nothing was going right. Why hadn't she insisted Roy take her and the suitcase back to Hembin and out of this disaster of a mess?

At any rate, it was too late now. She was quite tangled up, and all alone.

She weighed the options of coming clean to Arthur and the rest, but knew, despite their pacifist talking points from the morning, they would send her away, or possibly even send for the authorities. A girl as poor as herself could be sent to prison for stealing a suitcase, or for a misleading impersonation.

An 1870s Victorian prison was nowhere any girl should ever want to be. Indeed, diseases ran rampant in jails and dungeons. Prisoners were neglected and abused, even, at times, tortured, and they died all the time in England; jails were cheaper to fund with fewer people in them. The judicial system was so corrupt that she may never see the light of day again, once committed. A prison sentence would be a death sentence, and her death would most assuredly be premature.

She simply had to steal the watch. She was in too deep.

She pulled the fluffy covers over herself and could not help but fall into a deep and consoling sleep, only to be woken well after sunset by the hard knocks and raised voice of a concerned Arthur Prickwhile, asking if she was dressed and ready for dinner with Lady Huntron.

CHAPTER SEVEN

The Second Day—Evening

"No, no. I've fallen asleep. Let me dress quickly!" Mary shouted through the door toward him, throwing off her morning dress and then scrambling for her evening clothes, and ultimately attempting to tighten the corset herself.

"Shall I assist you?" came his muffled voice through the closed door, and she stopped where she was.

"Assist me in *dressing?*"

"My darling, it was a joke. Hurry, now. Only ten minutes till we're seated."

She smoothed her hair in the mirror and pinched her cheeks, then threw on Agnes's blue satin dress with ruffles and sleeves that cupped her entire shoulders. She did not know if it was acceptable as dinner attire, but she had no time to consult Antoinetta. As soon as she started struggling toward the door, she knew something was very, very wrong. The dress was six inches too long. She groaned toward the sky, then laughed. What was another little problem along the way?

She swung the door open, pocketing her key, and grabbed the corner of her dress and held it to walk. Arthur was standing a short way off by the stairs where he had been waiting for her, every golden hair perfectly combed. His pocket watch's chain glistened on his vest in the lamplight. He heard her and turned to face her.

"Your hair. It's wild."

"I'm sorry, I slept too long."

"I like it," he said almost too quietly, a bit raspy, and she took his arm. Once again, she was his object, and she didn't know quite what to make of it.

A typical man, Arthur did not notice the length of Mary's dress, but when they got to the Sunshine Room to have a small drink before dinner, it was the first thing that Antoinetta and Mrs. Singh pounced on her about, though in two very different tones.

"Mary Agnes, tomorrow we must spend the day sewing! This will not *do*. This dress is trailing behind you, sure to become soiled." Antoinetta clicked her tongue in a now-familiar gentle scold.

"Indeed, Miss Riboneaux, it's almost as if the dress were made for an entirely different woman," Mrs. Singh remarked, and Mary thought she saw the petite woman sporting a cold smile. The dimness made it very hard for Mary Potts to tell. At any rate, our Mary had regained her confidence. The worst thing that could have happened already had occurred: she had been found out. This led her to feeling a bit indestructible. She had chosen, in a sense, to not let Mrs. Singh have the upper hand, to retain her mystery, and to fight back.

"I sent off for my dresses recently. There must have been an error in the measurements. The violet ball gown is the only one I tried on at the seamstress shop, and I do recall her hemming it considerably."

"A simple error, and not without remedy," opined Mr. Singh.

Her heart softened toward him again. His pinky finger electrically brushed her palm as he handed her a glass of champagne and they briefly exchanged a smile; Mary wondered if Benjamin Franklin's key had smiled similarly at his kite when it was struck by lightning, the way she was gushing at being struck by love.

"To our new friend."

Mr. Singh raised his glass, eyes locked on her, and they all toasted Mary, some more enthusiastic than others.

Could it be possible that she was now also the subject of a toast among rich dandies and quaintrelles? She blushed crimson and smiled wide. Yes, tonight she would have fun, and nobody could stop her. Well, perhaps Walt Corning could put a damper on things just a bit with his underwhelming blandness, but even so, she would try to barrel through and make tonight just as memorable as the one before.

~

The young people were soon allowed into the ornate, dim dining room, where they were seated at the great, long table at impossibly fancy settings, leaving the head of the table free for Lady Huntron when she arrived. Mrs. Singh took the spot to the left of the head of the table, and Antoinetta on the right. Next to Mrs. Singh was Mr. Singh, and then Walt Corning at the end. Mary Potts sat between Antoinetta and Arthur.

She was thankful Walt Corning was not beside her, and also glad that Mr. Singh was directly across from her as she was drawn to him and hoped for more conversation, or even the chance to impress him, odd and infantile as it sounded. She was unable to stay angry at him, much as she tried.

It was not long before Lady Huntron entered the room in a grandiose way, wearing a blue evening gown that was well out of style. Her white hair fluttered like feathers around a bejeweled hairpin, and exaggerated earrings made her stretchy lobes sag. Despite the obvious signs of her advanced age, the woman retained a form of regal beauty that only those bred into high society could emit.

Mary stood as did the other guests.

"Lady Huntron, this is Mary Agnes Riboneaux, of Gr—"

"An honor to see you again, ma'am," Mary said, panicked that Antoinetta might say Greece. After all, who knew where the real Agnes was from?

Mary curtsied deeply. Antoinetta's eyes grew wide at the interruption, but then her face relaxed into a smirk. She probably assumed that Mary was nervous to meet the lady she'd snubbed last night. She'd never guess Mary's nervousness was really due to keeping up with her farce.

"I must apologize," Mary said, now, looking at Lady Huntron's somewhat stern visage. "I did not formally greet you at the ball last night. It was incorrect of me. In truth, I feared I would take you away from more important guests, and before I knew it, the time for the ball to end came upon me, and—"

Lady Huntron lifted her weathered hand to signal Mary to stop her excuses. One corner of her painted mouth drew up into a kind half-smile. "Don't worry yourself, dear. It's common to get wrapped up in things with a night as exciting as we had." Now, Lady Huntron raised her brows in warning. "I trust that at your next formal ball, you will not do the new hostess the same way. After all, not all of them are prepared to be so forgiving."

Mary exhaled. Lady Huntron, swimming in wealth as she was, was quite understanding and kind. This was going very well indeed.

"I give you my word, ma'am, that I will greet every hostess from now on. Again, I am sorry."

"That pleases me." She smiled fully and genuinely now. "Please, take your places. All of you," she said, and then to a waiter, "The first course can be served."

Mary relaxed her shoulders. It seemed that she was off the hook, for the dimness of the room, perhaps paired with Lady Huntron's poor eyesight and memory, allowed Mary to be inconspicuous as possible—or at least, she hoped.

Half an hour went by with Lady Huntron talking mostly to Antoinetta and Indira about small, unimportant things: distant relatives, décor, fashion, so-and-so's deliciously fat baby. The three men were engaged in further talks of hunting traps and game, leaving Mary alone with her thoughts and her scrumptious first plate—a clear soup with the rich flavor of onion and slow-boiled bone, and crusty bread.

A silence settled upon the table as the group realized they must eat instead of excitedly chatter.

It was Lady Huntron who next broke the quiet spell, questioning her handsome Indian guest about the rule that England exerted over India.

"And Mr. Singh, how goes the British Raj? Are the English treating you well?"

Both Arthur and Mr. Singh chuckled uncomfortably, exchanging a brief look, then Mr. Singh spoke. "My lady, I wish I could say so."

"Ah, but are the English so hard on your people?"

"Not all of them ma'am," he said, "and your great-nephew is especially kind to all Indians. There is the problem, you see, of the English treating the Indians as inferiors, and then there is institutional corruption. Such as when the British give the Indians unjust sentences in court while getting away with their own crimes all the time, and this is just one example. I am vexed to say, at times, there is even murder."

The space between Lady Huntron's eyebrows reduced to a deep, vertical crease. "I am saddened to hear this, but happy to know you find my great-nephew kind. He'd better be. Anyone inheriting this must do it the highest justice." She droned out this last part while waving her hand around to signal the great dining room. "Miss Riboneaux, do you find my Arthur to be kind?"

Mary set her fork down and glanced briefly at Arthur whose eyes betrayed that he was wondering the same thing. He looked almost innocent. "Oh yes, very."

"Well, he certainly seems very excited about *you*," Lady Huntron said, and then, "You know, it is hard to believe that you are little Agnes. You were such a blonde little girl. Now your hair is blacker than a raven."

"Yes, ma'am, curious thing." Mary looked down and took another bite.

"And I wholly remembered your eyes being bl—"

"Hazel, yes," Mary interrupted, "almost green. But they darkened. We've consulted a physician. It *is* common."

At this comment, Mr. Advik Singh stifled an outburst of laughter, and then made like he was coughing into his napkin.

Lady Huntron continued. "It is even harder to believe that it has been over twenty years since I saw you at—"

"With my parents at our home, indeed. I don't remember it, but they tell me you came and speak of it still." Now, Mary was taking a lot of risk as it occurred to her that one of Agnes's parents, or both, might be dead, and Lady Huntron might recognize the inconsistency.

"And are your parents well?" This question of Huntron's meant Agnes's parents, to Lady Blanche's knowledge, were still alive.

"Yes, ma'am," Mary said and quietly exhaled her tension. She had passed the test. The conversation drifted onto other things, and eventually people started chatting with those closest to them.

Mary fell delightfully into conversation with Mr. Advik Singh, who told her all manner of things about India: what one does at certain times of day, the different types of entertainment and deportment available to the younger crowds, more about the castes. It was factual talk, nothing personal, but Mary was enthralled that there could be other worlds so different from her own, where the people thought and dreamed the same as her, and where the people were so beautiful, so smooth, so lusciously built, as Mr. and Mrs. Singh.

"And what kind of sweets do you have there?" she asked him as the dessert pudding was served.

"Oh, by far my favorite is kulfi. It's ice cream. I shall take you there one day myself so you can try it."

The warmest smile spread across his handsome face. Mary's heart fluttered within her chest.

Mary Potts, this man is married.

Just then, Arthur's warm and masculine left hand slid under the tablecloth and rested on her inner thigh, giving it a slight squeeze. Who was this bad man trying to claim her, who couldn't stand her having a conversation with any other? She glanced at his face, and he gave the same smirky half-smile as when he had touched her foot secretly in the carriage. She was learning that he definitely liked secretive affection. He was so very good-looking; she could not decide if she wanted him or not.

"I shall retire," Lady Huntron announced, rising from the table and calling her chambermaid near to escort her. "I have not been well for several days, but today has been the worst of it. I need to lie down. I thank you for your company. The youth does these old bones good."

They all rose and bid her farewell. Mary was thrilled to have escaped the Lady's questions unscathed. Perhaps there wouldn't be any more questions during future meetings with the kind, old dame. Once the door had closed behind Lady Huntron, the young group of twenty-somethings smiled energetically at one another, seeing that they were now left alone, and it was not yet nine o'clock.

Fun could be had.

The table was soon abandoned in favor of the garden, at Antoinetta's suggestion. But once there, Mary shrunk away from the crowd and went to sit on a little stone bench among daffodils. It was not long until, in the dark of the evening, a man made his way toward her, and when close enough she recognized him as Mr. Singh himself, and she grew breathless, but only for a moment.

"May I?" he asked, sitting beside her, his inner peace extending to her and calming her nerves. They sat in silence for a few moments, watching the others chat and laugh from a distance in the outdoor lantern light. Mr. Singh looked as if he wanted to say something, then hesitated.

"Do you have something to say, sir?" Mary asked him.

He took out his pipe and matches. "Yes. Yes, I do." He lit it.

"Then please, do not hold back."

"It's only..." He took a drag. "I just want you to be very careful with the likes of Arthur Prickwhile. He knows exactly what he is doing. My fear is that you do not."

"How can you say such things? You are his friend!" Mary was truly surprised. She longed to ask him why he was concerned about a man playing with her heart, when he had done the same thing. But she decided that was a question for a different day. She would blow her cover if he knew she was also the soot girl from the pub.

Mr. Singh exhaled smoke slowly and elegantly into the sky. "I am his friend; that is why I can say such things. Such *honest* things." He stood, intending to stroll back to the group, but Mary stopped him from her place on the bench.

"Mr. Singh, can I ask why you have such a personal interest in my safety?"

At this he sighed, obviously tormented. "Let me speak plainly, as life is very short, and opportunities are few. Mary Agnes, you and I have a certain spark between us. I know you have felt it, too, with the brushing of my hand against yours or the like. I have only had this sensation a few times before, but consistently with you. What I want to know is why we are charged in this way. Does God want us to be friends? Or lovers? Or is it a sign we should stay far away from one another? I have no answers, but I am seeking. I believe that in your book it says, 'seek and ye shall find.'"

Mary's heart was a potent drum inside her chest. What was this man trying to achieve? And he was bold enough to quote the Bible in his analysis of their reaction to one another. He was quite brazen, indeed.

The thought crossed her mind that there was no possible way Mr. and Mrs. Singh were married; if they were, he could not and would not talk this way.

Surely not.

Perhaps they were courting, or engaged and simply calling themselves married. Or on the other end of the spectrum, perhaps they had already filed for divorce and were waiting for a judgment, and saving face in the meantime by acting as if everything were fine between them.

Mary knew she had to get to the bottom of this, so she decided to be direct. "And does Mrs. Singh know about this?"

He flashed his ivory grin and let out a breathy, smoky chuckle. "Yes, and she doesn't like it."

～

That night Arthur Prickwhile walked our Mary Potts indoors with the intention of escorting her to her room. As they made their way up the staircase, Mary could not fight the doubt nagging at her conscience. She had to know if her inkling about the Singhs' marriage was true, because if it was, there might be hope for her after all.

"Arthur, dear," Mary said, and Arthur paid her full attention immediately after being called a pet name. "I have a question for you. An obvious one, really."

"Ask me anything, Mary, and I will answer you as truthfully as I am able."

"I want to know if..." Mary trailed off, suddenly considering herself quite silly. She swallowed back the feeling and went on, "If Advik and Indira are indeed married."

Arthur laughed and blushed, which she had never seen him do, even during his most forward advances.

"Of course, the Singhs are married," he said after a brief, but nonetheless, alarming hesitation. "I was at the wedding." He darted his eyes from her face and slightly smiled, fidgeting with the handkerchief adorning the pocket of his coat.

Her pulse pounded audibly inside her head as her heart picked up speed. So, it appeared to be true despite their odd pairing. Now, she absolutely *had* to believe it, whether or not she liked it. And she did not like it. Not one bit.

She did not like that Mr. Singh was married, but she disliked even more that he was such an outrageous flirt, being already taken.

She worked at hiding her disappointment as they reached the guest hall, after which they promptly approached her door. When she opened it, Arthur waited again, insinuating his desire for an invitation.

"The time, Arthur?" she asked him, entering the room and again bringing the door between them.

He drew out his golden pocket watch and flipped open the top. "It's half past eleven." He stored it away in his vest pocket; she saw exactly how, and her heart ached. She was not sure if she could bring herself to do wrong to someone so smitten with her. She had never had any trickery in her. But if Declan told the truth about her the consequences could be dire. Her whole life was at stake. This game was getting much too complicated for her liking.

"You look sad," Arthur observed. "What's come over you?"

"I simply have a lot of things to think about."

"You might let me in, and I can counsel you." He smiled devilishly, but she knew his game. Mr. Singh had warned her about him and thought her naïve, but it was he that could not see the evil she must do to Arthur.

Seeing it was a rejection again, Arthur said, straightening his coat, "Twice is fine, Mary Agnes. But I will tell you, I do not want to be on this side of the door every night this week."

Mary's head spun. *The nerve!*

What a forward, pushy, insolent man. She would not let her scandalization be shown on her face. She pulled herself together and spoke calmly. "Don't worry, my Arthur. When the time is right." She smiled, still hurting inside, knowing she had to get that watch, even if it meant empty promises and teasing.

"When the time is right," he repeated, and squeezed her hand before walking off to his own bed chamber.

CHAPTER EIGHT

The Real Agnes Riboneaux

Poor, poor Agnes. Prepare yourself for a tale of misery and misfortune so bleak it is difficult to imagine all of the happenings affecting one singular person, and all in sequence to one another. I, Rutherford Wells, will try just as hard to do the story justice as I will not to laugh.

Having set out from the outskirts of London before the sun ever rose on Thursday, April 7, 1870, Agnes Ann Riboneaux traveled four-and-a-half painstaking and bumpy hours in a carriage until, when reaching the gateway town of Hembin, it was determined that the buggy had a serious problem with an axle and two of its wheels, which had caused the poor conditions of the trip.

The driver, one Richard Bell, whom her parents had hired as she was still under their care as an unmarried twenty-two year old, and who was also a personal acquaintance, and who was supposed to chaperone her at the ball, had no choice but to arrange to send her on to Mannerley in one of the public carriages instead, the drivers of which exacted a fee from each of the passengers, piling luggage and personal items on the back of the carriage.

There were numerous carriages such as these passing between Hembin and Mannerley Town, especially since it was such a festive weekend, and many of the working class would travel to Mannerley within the next three days for a chance at seeing the dashing Arthur Prickwhile or any number of the nobles who were to attend the ball, as many of them arrived early to settle in and rest before the event.

"You may have to travel with some individuals of the lower class," Richard Bell had told her, "but they shan't bite you."

While Richard repaired his axle what he could, and arranged for Agnes's carriage ride to Mannerley Town, Agnes took some coffee and toast in a shabby little establishment called The Drabbe Inn and Pub. There, she obtained some paper and penned a quick letter to her parents telling them of the change in plans, and copying her lodging information for their further correspondence: H.A.H.A. Which stood for Huntron Avenue Holiday Apartments, in Mannerley Town. She had reserved room number twelve which overlooked the shopping streets, where she could watch the pomp of the processionals, and it was said a good number of other fine people would also be lodging there.

She had no desire to make any sort of grand entrance but was honored to be invited to Lady Huntron's springtime ball, and hoped to meet a suitor, having a modest but satisfactory amount of money to her name. She did hope whoever she met would like a long girl, as she was a head taller than any of her male friends from home.

On Friday, April 8, before the party, she would go to the beautician to have her long blonde hair trimmed, indulge in a manicure, and perhaps even purchase a new set of earrings or a new pair of gloves. Agnes was good with money, and was not keen on blowing it away. She also was not a social climber, so she did not feel the need to impress the nobility as some of the more desperate girls would do, although her own violet dress was extravagant; she had purchased it at her mother's request and not of her own particular liking.

But for now, she handed the letter off to a freckled waiter and the money for postage. She watched him drop it into the letter sac that was to be taken to the postal office—it was still only nine o'clock. And before long Richard Bell was calling her out toward the public buggy.

Excited to get on with her trip, she paid the waiter and set off a bit too quickly, hitting her head hard on the low-lying medieval beams of The Drabbe's front entrance, which made her dizzy. She barreled blindly through the door and onto the path, but tumbled her lanky self into the sludge, looking much like a newborn giraffe.

"Good heavens, Miss Agnes!" Richard ran over quickly to assist her. All she could say, and think was, "Oh, no!" over and over.

Up she stood after a moment with only her pride really hurt, though her traveling dress was irredeemably soiled with large patches of mud and a small rip at the knees. It had not been a nice dress anyway, being made of plain gray fabric, but it was comfortable. Now she certainly fit in with the lower class that she would be traveling with.

The driver of the public buggy became impatient. "We're on a schedule, you know," he spat out bitterly.

Richard scurried over to the buggy, supporting Agnes with his arm. "Yes, of course. Let me introduce you. This is Miss Agnes Rib—"

"Alright, load 'er up," said the new driver, balding and in patched-up clothes. "This your'n?" He pointed to a cloth satchel Agnes held in her arms. Inside were her fine silk heels for the ball, dyed violet to match her dress, and all her money to pay for her stay at the H.A.H.A. and any food or shopping she wanted to do meanwhile, as well as travel and leisure expenses, like correspondence.

"Yes, but I'll keep this with me."

He scoffed at her. "No, you won't. Give it 'ere."

He took it out of her hands and meek, sweet Agnes did not protest, for she thought that if she alluded to the value of the contents, one of the poorer folks she was traveling with could wield it from her hands, or threaten her with a blade for it, or any number of things she had read and seen that the poor might do.

"There's little room inside the cabin, especially for extra bags," the driver said, and went around back of the carriage to load up her trunk and her money bag securely behind iron bars, and Agnes inspected it to make sure it was so.

She breathed deeply and said goodbye to Richard Bell, who apologized again for the conditions under which she must travel.

"It will be a very short trip. Two hours is nothing," he said, consoling her, though she needed no consolation.

Agnes could deal with this, and more, if she knew an evening of relaxation awaited her at her apartment and the next day becoming beautiful enough to enjoy the ball.

The streets were rather clear that day, and Richard had gone in to take his own coffee and breakfast before driving, or rather bumping, back to the outskirts of London to a man he knew to see about getting it properly fixed, so as it were he missed the whole unfortunate proceeding.

Agnes had loaded up between two chubby women and had a small babe placed on her lap. Her knees hit those of one of the four or five boys on the row across from her. In total, there were eleven people in the tiny cabin of the buggy including children, the eleventh person being a mischievous boy who jumped into the carriage as it was taking off, having been late because he was removing screws from the back of the wagon's iron luggage cage—which I have on good authority. Of course, this was unknown to noble Agnes. He just did it for fun and because he could sell a screw for a half-penny apiece at market.

It so happened as the wagon started off, as confirmed years later by a witness, that the screws were removed in such a way as to create a gap between the platform and the cage, and the shaking of the contraption with travel allowed the trunk and money bag to shimmy out little by little and finally plop onto the dusty streetside of Hembin, where soon a large red velvet curtain was tossed out a window by a woman who was eliminating clutter, falling right on top of the suitcase and the money bag, obscuring them completely from view.

Shortly after, the woman's husband, tasked with removing the junk from the streetside to the rubbish heap, began loading the items in the cart, when he saw the Portmanteau with beautiful initials and shiny bronze clasps.

"Are quite *all* of these things to go to the dump, my dear?" he called up to his wife.

"Would I throw something out the window onto the street among piles of other detestable things, in order to preserve it? Come now, Harry, use your brains!"

"It's just that *some* of these things look indeed very nice," he called again.

"No, no, no! Harry, your taste is disastrous. They are old things. Cart them off and throw them out!" Now her temper boiled, and her tone was more than direct.

"As you wish," mumbled the husband, and into the trash cart went the suitcase, the curtain, and many other old things, including kitchen scraps. He pushed the heavy cart up the sidewalk with great effort and the curtain threatened to slide off as he turned the corner where The Drabbe Inn and Pub was located, with the garbage dump behind it. He grabbed the velvety curtain quickly and slung it back up, not realizing the money bag had slipped off the cart when the curtain had started its descent. He rounded the corner and was seen no more until about ten minutes later when he brought a light and empty cart back home, having left all the rubbish and paid Roy his fee. All this before nine-thirty in the morning.

Of course, the sidewalk was cleared of the money bag by the time of his return home, because a pack of excited little boys just happened to be running amuck and skipping their first lessons of school that day. The leader of them had just grabbed the sac without thinking and then they slung it around to each other like a ball, having a grand time, and the same leading boy ended up with it inside his own school bag later in the day.

That night when the boy got home, as I've come to confirm by my own means, he untied the knot and saw the money and danced with joy. The dyed violet shoes he threw into the countryside latrine. And we all know where the traveling trunk ended up, and who took possession of it. It turns out that one person's serendipitous luck is another person's grievous misfortune.

Agnes, yes, back to Agnes.

There is one particular thing in life that produces a sort of placid somnolence in a person, and that is holding a sleeping baby. The infant on Agnes's lap fell into a deep sleep as the carriage trudged up and over and down the hills of Mannerley one after the other, and it was not long until Agnes's eyes also closed, as she was cradled between the two fat women and warmed to steaming with all the bodies in the cabin of the carriage. When she awoke, the carriage had pulled up to Mannerley Town. Indeed, two hours was nothing. And she was glad to have been asleep to not smell what she now smelled. It was a soured, putrid, digestive smell that permeated the air.

All the travelers hopped out one by one as did Agnes with the sleepy baby.

"I'm very sorry about that, miss," the mother of the baby said, taking it back in arms.

At first, Agnes wanted to ask what she was sorry about, but she stopped her words when she looked at her chest and saw that the infant's mushy nappy had leaked a mustardy brown liquid all down her bosom. She would indeed not escape the smell.

At any rate, Agnes, kind as she was, tried to stay positive and explained that she could easily rinse it and change at the H.A.H.A., and that the young, plump mother should not feel badly about it at all.

Down came the driver and heaved out all the luggage from the back platform. The people collected their things and went about to their respective accommodations.

"Where's mine?" Agnes asked patiently, knowing there must be an explanation.

"Is it not there?" The man inspected the platform, shaking his head. "Not good. Not good a'tall," he said under his breath.

Agnes stood, dumbfounded. The road and the carriage were now both very, very empty. The man grabbed the iron cage and wiggled it.

"I think your luggage must have slipped outta 'ere."

"When? Where?" Now Agnes grew alarmed. Her clothes. Her invitation. *Her money in its entirety.*

"Dunno, miss. Anywhere along the road from Hembin." Now, Agnes was fretting. She paced and fidgeted with her nails nervously.

"Alright, let's be logical. I'll just ride back in the carriage with you to Hembin. I'll take a window seat and watch for it the whole way. Once at Hembin if it is not spotted before, I will ask around, especially at the pub where I took my breakfast."

"That should work," the driver said, beginning preparations for his return trip.

"Good, then I'll just—"

"It's half a shilling to Hembin from 'ere," he said as he tweaked the harness on one of the horses.

"But, but I haven't any money. It was in the luggage."

"Then I'm sorry, miss."

But his tone communicated that he wasn't sorry at all. Now, people were approaching, and he received their payments and loaded up the carriage with their belongings. Soon it was full, and Agnes watched with her jaw dropped in disbelief as the horses started and the buggy took off without her.

This was Thursday, midday.

She knew for certain that the H.A.H.A. would sort this matter out. Despite being spattered with baby feces and having muddy, ripped skirts, she raised her head high and set out walking into town, and found Huntron Avenue and then the Holiday Apartments. She went inside and asked to be checked in, and they found her confirmed reservation. However, as she had no payment, the reservation could not stand. Before her very eyes, the room was given away to one of several people inquiring about accommodation.

Thursday, she spent sitting outside, trying to be the optimist that she was, but a late evening rain shower left her cold and wet. She slept on a tiny hill of dirt that seemed perfect for a pillow. When she woke, she had small, red ant bites all along her arms, chest, and face. Then the fear set in, and she cried hard.

Friday, she decided to go about and ask for help, but got little more than a loaf of bread and a glass of water. With her dirty dress, her pock-marked face and body, her stench, the bruise on her forehead from the beam, and her tears, she was not welcomed in the nice establishments and anyone with class was frankly quite scared of getting near her for fear of catching some dreadful contagious disease. To make matters worse, her hair, which was normally fine as a duckling's down and needed a daily wash to retain its healthy sheen, was weighed down by her own natural bodily oils and matted greasily to her head. Sweet, good, docile Agnes was without recourse and was beginning to panic.

On Saturday, the day of the ball, Agnes very nearly lost her mind. She had slept the night before under a parked carriage as the door was locked and she could not get inside. She had seen the Prickwhiles taking a stroll through the grounds on Saturday morning after breakfast and ran up to the gate desperately, shaking it with her hands, screaming that she needed to speak to Lady Huntron who would sort it all out. Arthur Prickwhile called two strong footmen to deal with the lunatic, and the two men quite thoroughly threatened her and physically removed her when she frantically attempted to climb the gate.

After this, she sat on a street corner begging for change from passers-by who had come to see the pomp of the ball. She was able to scrape enough money together to buy either paper and a stamp, or a biscuit with tea. Any letter she wrote would take several days to get to her parents, and it would take them a full day to travel to her. By her suffering, she calculated she would be dead in three or four days' time. So, she guzzled the tea and devoured the biscuit, though she had to do so on the walkway in front of the restaurant because the proprietor had said, "We don't serve your kind inside."

After this, she went about miserably, took a short nap in a graveyard, which was the only solitary place, for the crowds were forming. Then that evening, she watched the procession of arriving guests in tears, moaning aloud, wailing, and sobbing. "Oh woe, woe is me," she would cry. It was odd, because the people were packed in tightly like sardines all along the street leading to Mannerley, but there was more than an arm's breadth anywhere around Agnes at all times. So untouchable, she was.

By Sunday afternoon, all the royal-watchers and other spectators had already left, and Agnes sat by herself, holding her knees and rocking back and forth next to a shoe shop on the main street. From her position on the ground, she could see the full Mannerley Estate, but nothing had happened other than a girl had taken a run in a floral dress and the boy Prickwhile had followed her with two friends. But Agnes had been threatened plainly to not speak to them again. It was no use. So, she sat and rocked.

Now her mind was completely gone, and she talked to herself incoherently and the spittle ran out of her mouth and onto her chin, and ultimately into her matted hair. She rolled over onto her face. She did not want to see anything else, though she did hear the small crowd's crunching steps heading up Mannerley's front drive.

～

Roy Hicks was tired. He hadn't slept at all and had rushed to Hembin and back in the span of only several hours. However, it was all worth it to watch his dear Mary Potts walk off on the arm of a beautiful lady friend with two gentlemen friends willing to carry her—or Agnes's—trunk, and she herself dressed as she ought to be, and not as a barmaid. His heart was entirely warm at the good he had done.

He started his horses and pulled around and onto the main street as the four young folks neared the entryway of the estate in the far distance, carrying the trunk. The town was very empty and forlorn, with most of the travelers having already left, and all of the partygoers relaxing in their hotels before leaving for home.

As his buggy went along, he spotted a very unstable-looking, dirty girl, now lying face down on the main street and sobbing deep sobs. Never one to let a person in need remain that way, Roy stopped his buggy and hopped down to engage the youth in conversation, and perhaps share with her some of Prickwhile's generous tip.

"Hello there," he said gently, approaching her as if to a wild animal.

She sat up and scurried against the wall. Then came her lunatic moaning. "The clothes! The money bag! Lost during my travels. The H.A.H.A., I was staying at the H.A.H.A., but they wouldn't let me in. Help! The ants. Oh, the baby poo. Oh, I've fallen, oh, my knees! They don't serve my kind here, no, they don't serve my kind! Prickwhile, right there, at arm's length, and yet he won't help. He sends the footmen to take me away!"

His father's heart was overcome with compassion. At the very least, he would need to get her back to Hembin and then arrange for the authorities to take her to hospital, or even an asylum. But alone on this street, she could not remain.

"Coming with me, you are," Roy said to the vagabond lunatic, gently grabbing her arm and leading her to the carriage. To his surprise, the senile girl did not fight, she only looked at him with great relief. "If you stop your crazy talk and pull yourself together, I can even give you a job, a room, and board."

He loaded her on the back seat of the buggy and gave her of his own bread and water. She ate and drank monstrously, and then took a nap. When she woke, they were only half an hour from Hembin, and she seemed an entirely different person, having received a little food, a little drink, and a little love from humankind.

"Oh sir, please forgive my antics," she said, crying fervent tears. "You cannot imagine what my life has been these four days. You are my hero, my savior, my angel."

"Nonsense, child. The Lord put me in your path."

"Then blessed is He," she said, taking another swig of water.

"I'm Roy Hicks. Can I know your name at least?"

"My name is Agnes Riboneaux."

CHAPTER NINE
The Third Day

Mary Potts slept in, again, for now the second time in twelve years. How nice it was to swim around in the warm covers, which were not scratchy and woolen like those at The Drabbe, and seemed instead to be made of the softest, smoothest cotton available to man.

But no matter how nice the bedding, upon waking, Mary remembered the slowly rolling boil of her current predicament. In contrast to her normal life, now, her morning worries were not focused on innkeeping tasks, household chores, or children—though her heart did yearn for the little Hickses.

No. Now, she thought of all her lies, and how to keep up with them—and what might happen if she couldn't.

Her life of hard work had been so simple before all this. She remembered Briddie, and yearned for her. Briddie understood Mary, and did not accept excuses from her. She held her to the highest standard of honesty, despite her urging Mary to fake her identity for the ball. It had been the one and only time Briddie had ever encouraged malfeasance. It was true, Briddie had initially helped get Mary into this.

But she certainly didn't know it would lead to this mess.

And what would Briddie say now about Mary's plan to steal for slimy, scrawny, impotent Declan? And to take from a man who so desperately wanted her for himself? And how would she react to know that Mary was entertaining flirtatious fantasies about a married man? Our Mary Potts had deviated so far from her own standards, she could now very well be called by the name Mary Agnes Riboneaux, because she was certainly not herself.

She was roused by Arthur's soft and masculine voice from the door. She threw on Agnes's floral robe, breathing deep to muster her confidence, and opened the door, greeting him coyly.

"Sleeping late, I see?" he mused, giving her a weak but sultry smile.

"Is this wrong on a Monday?" Mary suddenly feared she'd broken a custom.

"No, my dear," Arthur said and laughed. "Especially not this week. You must do what you please."

Mary sighed, relieved. This was the Monday of Holy Week, after all. April 11.

"The fellows—they're waiting." Arthur shot a glance down the hall. "We shall spend the day with the dogs on a hunting expedition. We'll return for a bath and dinner later in the evening, though I shall be bone tired. And I wonder..."

Arthur's expression grew pleading, and Mary's heart picked up speed.

"If I might take your hand for just a moment, as it is Mannerley custom since the house's construction for any man heading out to sport to receive a token or an affection from the lady... who... he admires." Arthur paused and swallowed hard. "It is meant as a means of bringing good luck in the field."

"Yes, of course," she said and held her hand out, though without her glove. To her relief, he took no notice of her callouses, and pressed it to his heart. There she felt the hard outline of his antique golden watch under her hand. "May you be very lucky today, indeed."

He smiled his perfect, pearly grin. He had not shaved, and the golden-brown stubble suited his glowing face. "I only regret that we shall not spend much time together today. I hope you will not be bored." Arthur was... *sweet*.

"Not in the least. Antoinetta already has many plans laid out for me."

He brought his face close to hers, then laid his lips on her forehead, brushing away curls in the process. It was the first kiss he had given her, and it was protective; kind. "Goodbye, then."

"Goodbye."

Mary Potts had no sooner closed her door than she heard a knock and feared it was Arthur again, wanting to go much further than an innocent kiss of the face, overcome by passion as he frequently seemed to be, and impulsive at that.

"Mr. Singh?" Mary gasped when she opened the door and saw him. He stood there vulnerably with a longing look in his deep eyes. What could he want? And worse still, why was she excited to give him anything he asked?

You must go against your flesh, Mary.

She had in Arthur an unfathomably rich and handsome suitor who was dying inside of passion for her, and she liked him quite well, though there was the problem of pulling off the heist. Arthur was exciting to her physically, which is why she never fully rejected his advances. But Advik Singh was much deeper, much more thrilling intellectually and relationally. He awoke in her all kinds of happiness and dreams of contentment, and all her unspoken fantasies were satisfied when he asked her for a token of good luck.

"I don't think I'm the right person to give this," Mary said, now red in the face, going against her own wants. This could not be. She could not allow herself to do such a thing to Indira, much as she disliked her.

"But I think you are. Am I not the one who should decide such a thing?" Mr. Singh laughed.

Mary thought it must be a very passionless marriage for him to speak this way. The same question nagged at her: how could they be married, and he be talking this way?

"Please," he said and took her hand.

Electrifying, again. And this time it ran through her whole body several times, leaving her warm with a pounding heart. His chest heaved under his excited breaths.

Mary gained courage and pulled away. "No. I'm sorry Mr. Singh. Believe me, I am *very* sorry, and wishing the situation were quite different so I might follow my heart. But I will not do such a betrayal to another person. I have just given a token to Arthur. You can ask him what it was."

"Yes, I see," Mr. Singh said, his mouth turned downward at this rejection. "You shouldn't betray Arthur. You are right in this matter."

"I wasn't speaking of betraying Arthur," Mary said impatiently, appalled at how heartless he could be to his own wife.

At this, the sadness in his handsome visage grew more acute, and with it Mary's desire to forego all morality and console him and let him fully into her heart. Sensing her flesh was growing weak, she bid him farewell and closed the door behind her, more than a little grieved at the situation. If Indira hadn't even crossed his mind as a possible betrayal, he must not be as intelligent as she had perceived, or at least not near as considerate and loyal.

~

The three ladies, Mrs. Indira Singh, Miss Antoinetta Prickwhile, and a very troubled Mary Potts ate a quick lunch midday and then devoted themselves to the alterations of Agnes's dresses. As with any detailed work of the hands done in a group of young women, the conversation soon turned to romance.

"I just wonder when he will wake up," Antoinetta complained of Walt Corning. "We have courted since we were sixteen. That was nine years ago. He has never asked me to marry him, nor even hinted at the matter. I think he is quite comfortable. I admit, now that I see my other prospects such as the business and Mannerley, and enjoy such satisfying friendships, I do not feel a need to marry. But deep in every girl's heart is the desire to be desired. The desire to receive commitment."

Mary smiled, remembering. "I grew up seeing non-committed love, as you speak of, Antoinetta. But when my sister married, it all happened in the span of three weeks. They were so destined for one another, yet so determined to do right by one another morally. Nothing and no one could have stopped them from running to that church that day and saying their vows. They simply *had* to become one. It was the only satisfaction, the only fulfillment, of the deep and passionate longing within them."

"That is beautiful." Antoinetta shook her head. "Walt and I have gone so slow. How can I ever hope to attain such momentum?"

"And what is your sister's name?" Indira asked.

Mary hesitated, not fully trusting the small, mysterious woman. Finally, she chose to be honest.

"Bridget." To Mary's surprise, Indira smiled.

"So it is," she said, as if she knew, then wiped her face blank.

Mary picked back up her advice. "Perhaps, Antoinetta, you must introduce a bit of passion in the relationship. Perhaps not dress so matronly, or do something to incite his physical interests. Perhaps you could lay your hand on his more often, or lay your head on his shoulder."

"But certainly not lay his hand in your lap," Indira now said, eyes burning through Mary, and Antoinetta laughed at the notion.

How could Indira have known that Arthur had done this the night before under the table, squeezing her thigh, reminding her she was his date, not Advik's? Mary breathed out and brushed it off, regaining confidence.

"Nothing so forward, my dear Mrs. Singh, but I do figure that Antoinetta's relationship with Walt Corning has grown stale because it has lain dormant and passionless for far too long. And men are, after all, guided intensely by libido and eros. A little lowering of your collar, or a little showing of your ankles would do the trick." Mary Potts was quoting her own dear mother from one of the premarital lessons she had overheard her giving Briddie before her marriage to Roy.

Antoinetta guffawed and fanned herself, red-faced. "Oh, my dear Mary Agnes, this is entirely inappropriate. How you must carry on in Greece!"

"I agree, Antoinetta," Indira said condescendingly. "The Church forbids it, and it can bring no good, but a baby born in shame. I of course saved the physical aspect of marriage for after the wedding, and it has been a most blessed union. So happy are we that we can scarcely be apart, and when we are apart, we long for one another. I have never seen anyone in a happier marriage union than myself and my devoted Mr. Singh."

But Mary knew Mr. Singh was *not* happy, nor was he devoted as she said.

Mary gained courage and spoke directly, throwing caution, and consequences, to the wind. "Mrs. Singh, might I ask, are you and Mr. Singh *fully* married?"

An angry spark quickened inside Indira's eyes. "What a preposterously odd question. Of course, we are." Indira looked briefly at Antoinetta, eyes wide, and laughed in disbelief at Mary's inquiry.

"But *legally*?" Mary pressed, interrupting Indira's reaction.

"Mary!" Antoinetta scolded softly, scandalized. Her hand met her heart and clutched a locket she wore.

"Yes, legally," Indira answered, indignant. "If not, then I would be a fornicator or perhaps an adulteress if Mr. Singh was with another. And we couldn't have that, now, could we?"

Mary dodged her question; she knew what Indira was insinuating, but she still needed closure. "But are you having any issues with Mr. Singh, or are you thinking of divorcing? Because the marriage doesn't seem—"

"Enough!" Indira squawked. "We're very, very happy. Too happy, in fact. I have no need to defend my marriage to you. You have nothing to do with it. Your questions are speculative and offensive."

"Indeed, you are not behaving correctly as a lady should," Antoinetta said, disappointment in her voice. "Come, let us have a break. It's far too warm in here. Perhaps we can take a small walk to the rooftop veranda. The views are superb."

"No," Mary said, standing abruptly. The whole situation made her nauseated, and her stomach lurched. The dresses had been finished for some time, so she quipped an apology to Indira and thanked them both. Then she retired to her room, feigning tiredness, for she could not stand to hear any more about Mr. and Mrs. Singh's supposedly happy union.

Supposedly happy, though *definitely* a union.

And Mary resolved that the very next time she and Mr. Singh were alone, she would confront him about the matter. Until then, she'd have to continue hiding her dismay.

Because the situation was a scandal, indeed.

~

In the evening, a message was delivered to Mary's room saying that Lady Huntron had fallen ill and would be resting in her bedchamber in the west wing until further notice. Dinner would be a warm soup with bread and selection of cured meats and would be served when the men arrived from hunting and got cleaned up, which was not long in coming.

By seven o'clock, they were being served, and she was sitting at the end of the table with Antoinetta on her right hand and Mrs. Singh across from her. Next to Mrs. Singh was Walt Corning. Arthur and Mr. Singh were both as far as possible from Mary Potts. This occurrence, for some reason, made Mary sad. She was torn between wanting Arthur Prickwhile's secret, passion-inducing affections while they would last, and wanting the forbidden conversation and intellectual intimacy of the deep and so very satisfying Mr. Advik Singh. The married Mr. Advik Singh.

As Arthur rose from the table, he dropped the jacket he had slipped over the back of his chair. There was no need to impress as Lady Huntron was not dining there, and the youths were left to their own entertainment once again.

"Oh, how clumsy of me," Arthur said as Declan lifted his fallen garment from the luxurious ceramic of the floor.

"And your handkerchief, sir," Declan said, offering it, "and your pocket watch." He spoke this last part while looking directly at Mary Potts' eyes, and she remembered with heartache what she must do.

Arthur positioned his timepiece and patted it twice, then announced that he was leaving the dining room. "Mary Agnes, come with me," he whispered as he passed her chair. Just like an obedient puppy, she arose and followed him through the kitchen and stuffy adjacent sitting room, and into the library with its floor-to-ceiling cherry bookshelves packed with multicolor volumes and two large, green velvet sofas. She had no idea why she was following him. In a way, she wanted to know if he was really dangerous or not.

"It's practically soundproofed in here," he remarked.

Mary did not understand why there should need to be no sound. She backed up to the door, unnerved by this comment as she did not fully trust him.

He must have realized this from his place stoking the fire and apologized. "For the game we'll play. I believe Antoinetta wants charades and impersonations this time. Here we won't disrupt Lady Huntron's rest."

Mary relaxed.

"It will be a few minutes before they all come in. Here, recline with me." He took his place on a green sofa, leaning back, and propping up his legs on an ottoman. She sat cautiously beside him, but his warm arms soon enveloped her and brought her softly to his chest, which rose and fell with comfortable breaths. It was very nice to be there, and she grew cozy, but remarkably, she never felt the least bit safe. Her mind flitted to thoughts of what she must do to poor Arthur, and how she would love to be in this same scintillating position but with a different, forbidden man.

Arthur interrupted her thoughts with a sensual whisper. "Will you not look up at me and press yourself to me like you did while we danced, so that I might kiss you properly?"

A tingle ran through her. She rose to a less enticing position. "My dear, Arthur, I can't. Please do not make me reject you so much. When the time is right."

"Yes, yes, and it is not the right time." He sighed greatly and sat himself up just as Antoinetta and the rest of them came in, bringing with them glasses and a bottle of champagne, big smiles, and a desire to have fun. And that, they did. Charades and impersonations, of course, were Mary's specialties.

"Is she not delightful in this game?" Arthur asked, to rotund agreement, even from Walt Corning, who stated the obvious, saying that impersonations must be like the person they mean to copy in order to be funny, to which no one knew how to respond.

"I say, she is so good at faking, how can one know if she is ever being true?" This conjectured Mrs. Singh, and everyone laughed, but Mrs. Singh glared at Mary.

When the game was done the ladies stood by the fire. Antoinetta and Mrs. Singh talked of their private things in a low mumble. Walt and Mr. Singh were conversing near the door, ready to call it a night. Mary Potts realized that Arthur had curled up and fallen asleep on the sofa. She went up to her own room and fetched a light quilt. She removed his shoes and covered him with the blanket, and she removed his cufflinks and placed them in his jacket pocket. The watch was there in plain sight, but she did not take it. No, she did not steal it, yet.

Her eyes darted to Mr. Singh, who had grown uncomfortable with her services to Arthur. He looked at her with longing and pain from across the room. Mary's frustration rose within her. How could he expect her to return his advances and be romantically his, with him already taken? What kind of woman did he assume her to be? It was not to be borne. And soon, she would tell him so.

Silently, he turned from Walt and left the room, his broad shoulders disappearing into the penumbra of the foyer.

"What's got into him? We were in plain conversation," said Walt Corning.

"I think we should all call it a night, and let sweet Arthur rest," Mary whispered, and that is exactly what they did.

When Mary retired for the night, she found a letter on her pillow that she had not before noticed. It was from Declan Thobbs and read: *Good Friday (15th) is my day off and no one shall suspect me missing. I shall take you to Hembin myself and leave you at the Drabbe, then I shall go on to P. Lazáre to sell it and be done with this mess and all of you. We shall make our escape during Good Friday church services where they will all be in Mannerley Town. Do your part, and I will keep your secret. D. T.*

CHAPTER TEN

An Update on Agnes

When we last left poor, unfortunate Agnes Ann Riboneaux, she had been the object of the compassionate mercy of Roy Hicks, who, after asking her name, became tongue-tied from the shock of realizing who Agnes was, and how he had contributed to her demise.

"Are you quite alright, sir?" Agnes had asked after a moment, to which he had said yes. Then they rode in silence a little while, with Agnes only speaking once more to thank him profusely and pledge her devotion to repaying him, somehow. This was Sunday, April 10, Mary's second day at Mannerley.

Later, they had arrived at Hembin, and Agnes was instantly thrilled. How God was now working so mightily in her favor, she remarked, so that she was passing through the same town where all her great troubles had begun.

Roy introduced her to Briddie, whose reaction was a nervous, wide-eyed grin which he had fully expected, knowing all his wife's expressions well, and being quite familiar with this one that she used when she was caught in a tricky situation.

Briddie absolutely insisted that Agnes be bathed, her dress be scrubbed, and her pock-marked face anointed with medicinal creams. Briddie made Agnes rest in Mary's bed all afternoon and evening, and sleep there that night, her large feet hanging off the end. Agnes was grateful for the doting attention and the healing time of rest. On Monday, April 11, however—Mary's third day at Mannerley—it was hard to keep the rested and sprightly Agnes from finding out too much. She had asked both Roy and Briddie that morning at breakfast if they had seen a suitcase and a money bag, the loss of which had spiraled her into homelessness and pan-handling in the turn of one weekend. Roy, unable to lie, told the truth as best he could without really *telling* the truth.

"We've seen no money bag at all," he said, and it was true, "but it was said a suitcase was found and sent on to Mannerley, having an invitation to the ball within its contents." Briddie stomped his foot behind the bar where Agnes couldn't see.

"Oh indeed, it must be mine! I am so glad to hear it was found. But alas, I was dreadfully threatened and escorted from the premises while in my lowest state. I fear I am a *persona non grata* at Mannerley now. I will simply have to write to Lady Huntron herself and explain. At times the post is very quick, and this problem may be solved tomorrow or the next day. I must send word to my parents today to get more money. Do hired carriages travel near London? I can send the message that way."

Roy and Briddie looked at one another, and Roy knew he had to think fast to thwart Agnes's plan. "They *do*," he said, hesitating a bit while thinking how he could keep Agnes occupied and intercept her letter. "But, dear Agnes, let us reason. Your parents will be very unhappy indeed to hear about all these occurrences. As far as they know you are having a wonderful holiday in Mannerley Town. Let us keep them very much at peace by not involving them."

"You do make a valid point. It is quite a shameful situation. My father would be appalled. And my mother's nerves can't handle much."

"Indeed, think of your mother," Briddie urged, holding two drooling babies, perhaps to aid in sentimental persuasion.

"Give me your letter to Lady Huntron, and I will send it myself," Roy offered, careful to not give a timeline of when he would send it, as he planned to wait several days to buy time. "And what's more, I can hire you as a server and pay you a shilling and a half a day. In four days, you will have enough for your trip there and back as well as your return home. You should not have to ask your parents for anything."

"Yes, but in my bag were six crowns—that is thirty shillings. And now you will offer me only six."

Now, Roy appealed to her good nature. "Yes, but did you not say you owed me for rescuing you from destitution? Our hardest worker is absent this week, you see. She, er, well she had a commitment, so we are scrambling to cover her shifts. You can repay me by working, I will pay you and send your letter, and later you can go to Mannerley, after you receive word, and do as you have said."

At this Agnes smiled brightly. "It would be my honor to repay you in this way, by covering such a crucial need. I believe these four days will not be too long to wait. I should like very much to attend the Good Friday services at Mannerley Chapel with Lady Huntron. I shall mention this in my letter, and she will not deny the invitation. By Friday morning I will be at Mannerley, go to church, retrieve my luggage, pass through here again to say hullo and maybe stay a night, and be home again in time for Easter."

Agnes, having received a piece of paper from Briddie, went to work on her letter, which she gave to Roy, who stored it in his pocket. He would need to buy time and try to work out the puzzle of Mary's return and Agnes's departure. Then there was the obvious factor that Agnes would present herself at Mannerley, and Lady Huntron and the Prickwhiles thought Mary was Agnes. The lie, one way or another, would be exposed. The plan had always been for Mary Potts to secretly escape, leaving Agnes's things at Mannerley so no theft was involved, and then return to The Drabbe where she blended in and was unrecognizable. But now, Roy knew that was no longer possible, as Agnes knew him, and even Arthur Prickwhile had seen him and the beat-up carriage that read the name of The Drabbe Inn and Pub if the young man had cared enough to retain the information. By one means or another, he sensed that everything would come to a head, and it wouldn't be pretty.

And might I tell you, he wasn't wrong.

CHAPTER ELEVEN
The Fourth Day

The days in this tale may be running together, so I will take a moment to remind the reader that Mary's fourth day at Mannerley estate was Tuesday, April 12th, and on this particular day she woke with a headache caused undoubtedly by Declan's urging her to commit the heist.

She was summoned around ten by sweet-eyed Antoinetta, who said that Lady Huntron had requested the companionship of all three of Mannerley's young female guests at her sickbed for the morning. So, Mary Potts, Antoinetta Prickwhile, and Indira Singh dressed and ate quickly and reported to Lady Huntron's dreary room, where they reclined on a sofa together at her side, sometimes reading to her, other times maintaining small talk, and in general keeping the old woman company, though not without a bit of sadness for the sickly one. Lady Huntron's sagging skin was yellow and her eyes were framed with droopy, purplish bags.

When Lady Huntron dozed off and there was no longer a steady need to entertain her, all Mary's mind could do was weigh her options; she could focus on nothing else. Mrs. Singh, upon starting up new conversation with Antoinetta, commented how absent Mary seemed, and mused with a smirk that it may be love's doing.

"It's only a headache," Mary lied. Poor Mrs. Singh. Some clairvoyant she was. Mary questioned again just how much she knew.

"You must close your eyes," Antoinetta said, placing the back of her hand on Mary's forehead. "You don't feel hot. Nevertheless..." Antoinetta turned, raising her finger to a servant nearby. "An ice pack, please."

And when it was brought, Mary did as she was told, resting her head on the back of the green velvet sofa, and closing her eyes. Which, in turn, gave her the perfect opportunity to think everything out.

Here she was, pretending to be another. In time, the real Agnes, whoever she was, would somehow communicate with Lady Huntron, as she had been a personal invitee to the ball and to Mary's knowledge had never arrived. Why she had not written sooner to explain her situation was a mystery to Mary. When that inevitable thing happened, Mary would be exposed. And if she were exposed while still in the home, she could be accused of theft, for all of Agnes's things were in Mary Potts's possession, even though she intended fully to leave them cleaned and pressed for Agnes's retrieval—never mind that all her garments were now a full six inches too short.

If charges were filed and the authorities were to come, Mary could be thrown in prison. People were known to die in such circumstances. Her life could very well be over at only twenty-three years old, and all for a bit of flirting and fine living.

She needed to leave *before* Agnes communicated with Lady Huntron, and go back to The Drabbe, putting on her pale brown uniform and scrubbing the kitchen, where no one would ever find her, having her few secret days of flirtation forever in her heart. But how could she know when Agnes would write?

And Declan! Declan Thobbs was in charge of filtering all correspondence at Mannerley; he was the one who left each person's letters on their desks or on their pillows. He was the one who delivered all of Lady Huntron's letters to her bedside. It occurred to Mary that he, like herself, also did not want to be caught, as his desire was to leave Mannerley, sell the watch and collect the sum. As he had written, this escape was planned on Friday. And it was Tuesday.

Every day she stayed at Mannerley, every hour that went by, was a gamble. But with Declan on her side, she may be able to go through with the planned escape, as he would intercept any letter and not allow it to come to Lady Huntron, or so she hoped, as a letter from the real Agnes would also spoil his chance at selling the watch. Mary needed despicable Declan's protection, and Declan needed Mary's closeness to Arthur in order to fulfill his greed. It was a nasty sort of symbiosis that Mary could not believe she had become stuck in.

Her alternative, she considered, was much too risky: tell the truth and hope that Arthur was still mad about her, mad enough to still pursue her. She could marry him and take advantage of the comfortable life he could give her, though she did not love him. She wanted to laugh aloud at how silly it was, but stopped short so as not to draw attention to herself. It would never, ever work.

Men like Prickwhile were so consumed with appearances and rank. As soon as she confessed, he would drive her to the authorities himself; she would be shocked to find any compassion in him at all for a poor barmaid. His main interest in life was himself and what he could get out of those around him. Particularly what he could get out of women without an ounce of long-term commitment. Who was she kidding? He had no interest in marriage.

She had absolutely no choice. As much as she hated to do wrong to Arthur who had only lavished her with affection and praise, albeit short-term, she had to steal the watch, and she had to steal it soon. Friday was just around the corner.

~

The afternoon was drizzly, but Mary still decided to take a long stroll. She came in wet and chilled around four o'clock, and found the house quiet and dim from the low-hanging clouds. As she reached the top of the grand staircase, she heard soft footsteps coming her way, and then saw Arthur Prickwhile, dapper as ever, leaving his room and walking slowly but confidently toward her.

She met him at her door, unlocked it, and this time, against her better judgment, and solely for the purpose of robbing him, she let him in, saying a prayer all the while that he was not as malevolent as she sometimes supposed him to be. She would steal his watch, but she did not want him to steal anything from her in the process.

"You should change," he said softly, trailing a warm, rough finger down her upper arm to the peak of her elbow. She knew his game by now, and Mr. Singh had warned her.

"I think I'll just dry out by the fire." She moved there, holding out her cold hands. Of course, he trailed behind her, hands in his pockets, whistling a tune, scoping out his surroundings for the perfect seduction, and planted himself at her side where he stared into the lapping flames. A golden gleam danced on the watch chain and reflected on both their faces. He turned his body toward hers, but she pretended not to notice and continued her task of warming her hands. She glanced from the corner of her eye at the glistening chain. How on earth would she manage to undo it?

"You must face me, Mary Agnes," he said with a slight laugh.

"I must?" Mary Potts turned. His two strong hands gripped her slim waist.

"This dancing position reminds me of when I first loved you."

Oh, good heavens did he say love? Now she was really doing a bad thing.

Arthur leaned his face near hers so she could feel his breath, and she caught the softest scent of the grooming fragrance he must have used on his face after shaving.

Bay rum.

She had smelled it on many of the numerous male visitors to her mother's shack. Her mother, a gypsy traveler woman, had been disowned by her own family after Briddie was conceived. She set out for Port Lazáre and used some stolen candlesticks as a down payment on a little wooden shack right on the main street that jutted off from the port's primary docks.

It had a porch, and her mother would draw around thick white curtains to make a kind of salon. There, travelers, sailors, and pirates alike paid a pretty sum to have their fortunes told. And many times, the men who came for a double purpose and might care a bit what they looked and smelled like, stayed inside those heavy canvas curtains that swayed in the breeze a little longer than normal and with noticeably less conversation. And most times, that class of men smelled of bay rum.

Mary melted a little inside. She wondered if this fine room in Mannerley estate was her splintery wooden porch; if this handsome, rich aristocrat was her drunken swindler just passing through with a crown or two to squander. Was she all that different from her mother, doing an intimate thing for a shiny metal object like a coin, or perhaps a watch? Did Mary carry this trait from her mother in her blood? How could her mother have allowed herself to act in such a way?

Total abandon was the only logical answer to that question. And Mary would have to do the same if she wanted to save her own skin.

Mary focused on her task, and let herself go.

Arthur's brown eyes looked calmly down into hers as he breathed on her, and she breathed him in. She tilted her face up, and their mouths met and danced. As he grew in the intoxication of his passion, she lay her hand on his breast pocket, then silently and gingerly removed the watch chain from the buttonhole, and then obscured both watch and chain within her palm.

He moved her over to the sofa where he reclined her, never parting his lips from hers, running his hands all up and down the back of her corset, and onto her hips. Was he fumbling with buttons? Oh, could they be going so very fast? She quickly deposited the watch and chain between the cushion and the back of the sofa, and put both of her hands on his chest to push him off just slightly, but smiling sweetly so as not to communicate a rejection.

He sighed and sat up, hair disheveled. "Mary, Mary," he said, now rubbing his face, "I don't *want* to stop."

"But we must," Mary said, tears filling her eyes. Arthur took this the wrong way, never imagining that she was upset for having stolen from him, instead suspecting that he had scared her or gone too far. His lustful look abated and his face softened.

"Oh, you are a good and innocent girl, aren't you Mary? I have been foolish. I would have taken everything from you if you had let me. I must learn to control myself." Arthur spoke as if he had made this supposed mistake many times before. "You are not my wife, yet," he said.

Mary was shocked to hear him speak this way. She knew he wanted her, but could he really want her forever? Enough to pledge faithfulness, in sickness and in health? He could not really be so evil as she thought if he would consider a commitment. She was altogether confused. For a moment she thought she must tell him the truth, but she could muster no courage. His sad face looked sweet. Oh, how she wanted so badly to be in love with him. He would make her so comfortable and satisfy every physical need and desire she had.

He was obviously upset with himself and rose and walked out of the room, not looking again her way. "Good bye for now. And I am sorry." And with that, he left.

∼

That night Mary arranged to have her dinner delivered to her room, and sent her apologies to her friends. She could not face Arthur after the incident. To Mary's surprise, Antoinetta herself brought the tray in, just to be able to visit her a bit, as she had not seen her since earlier that morning, and she was brimming with her own troubles to talk about.

As she set the tray on the table and served Mary's drink, she commented along the way, "And when it was said you would not come, I told Declan I would take it to you myself. He gave me these two letters for you and told me to tell you he will be caring for Lady Huntron on the night shift tonight, so he will be out of reach, as she will not stand for any of her servants to take absence while she is down sick, though today she is feeling somewhat better. My brother said that your ill-feeling must be because of him. I dare say Mr. Singh tore into him after that. 'What have you done?' he asked him again and again, as if my brother were some sort of monster."

Antoinetta chuckled at the perceived absurdity.

Mary ate, both swooning over Mr. Singh's response to Arthur and with an intense desire to open the letters, but unwilling to allow Antoinetta to realize this. Antoinetta continued her talk. "Surely, he has hurt you in some way. Shall I talk to him or send for him, so that we might fix it? I truly despise hard feelings among friends. I long to make it right."

"Your brother has been nothing but affectionate to me," Mary Potts admitted.

"So, you *do* love him?" she asked, her blue eyes growing wide.

I love the way he looks, she wanted to say. *I do not love him.*

"I decline to answer anything like that. My mind is tired. I have only known him for a few days."

"Yes, you are being very realistic. I think it is smart to not get your heart too involved. Time will tell. But with my Walt, I must ask for some guidance. I have tried what you said, introducing physical touch. First his hand, then my head on his shoulder. And he has responded all too well. Today he placed his hand on the small of my back, and he kissed me warmly, as when we were teenagers. I regret that Mrs. Singh will not think very highly of me for this. But I am learning that in Greece they must know more of the heart than we do here in the Queen's land. I feel a proposal might not be long in coming. Or at least I hope."

Then, thinking, she asked, "Do you find Walt so very dull?"

Mary searched for words and tried not to let her face betray how silly she found Walt. She certainly didn't want Antoinetta to think she was laughing at her. Finally, she came up with a very political answer. "What a person speaks is not a reflection of all the complexities of their mind, Antoinetta. And since he speaks so little..." Oh, dear. Was she saying now that he had no complexities in his mind?

Antoinetta did not catch the slight. "Yes, you are right. Of course. And I do love him. He is stable and kind."

"Those are two very important qualities." Mary nodded reassuringly.

"And he loves me, which is more than I can say of most. I never received such attention from men as you. People always remarked on my pleasantness, but it was never something that drew in the fellows." She laughed. "I've been told by trusted advisors that my chin is lacking regal definition. I like my chin, just the same."

"Do you think I receive much attention?" Mary was surprised.

"Well, yes, Mary Agnes, I do. You are breathtaking in your appearance, unusual, even. Mrs. Singh even says so, and she does not praise just anyone. My brother is ready to make you his own, and Mr. Singh, well, Mr. Singh betrays his true feelings for you though he would hide them. My Walt, of course, is committed to only me." Really, Walt was like a toad on a log and could not be expected to become excited about anything.

"Mr. Singh!" Mary now exclaimed, pausing her meal. "I don't know how they do things in Calcutta, but it seems all wrong to me."

"Do you think they are so very different from ourselves?" Antoinetta asked.

"Yes, I do! The way he treats Indira..."

"Ah, but Mary, it is to be expected. So many years around the same person. Perhaps you don't understand that dynamic."

"Now you defend the behavior?" Mary was upset and quickly losing her appetite. "Antoinetta my dear, I need to rest."

"Of course. My, you really are cross today, aren't you, Mary Agnes? I shall tell my brother it is all due to your mood and nothing he did. For now you have become angry with me, and for very little." She rose and headed to the door.

"Forgive me," Mary said, composing herself.

Antoinetta paused for a moment, then her face relaxed gently. "We all have bad days. Please rest. And be kinder tomorrow."

Out she went, and Mary tore into the letters.

CHAPTER TWELVE

The Fourth Day—Letters and Night

To Agnes Riboneaux; Guest at Mannerley Estate
From The Drabbe Inn and Pub, Main Square, Hembin
April 11, 1870

Dearest "Agnes",

It may be of interest to you that A.R. is now employed at The Drabbe for one and a half shillings per day. Roy rescued her, as she was in a dire way in Mannerley Town, all from our doing, indirectly. As a thank you for this rescue, she is working for us for four days. She will write to Lady Huntron about attending church services this Good Friday, and when she receives word, she will travel there. It is important that you disappear before the letter arrives. Roy is trying his best to entertain her and keep her busy, but it has been only one day, and she is very interrogative. He has intercepted her letter to Lady Huntron, while promising to send it. It is in his coat pocket. He will hold off as long as he can. She has already asked him once today if her letter is in the mail, and as you know, he is unable to fully lie. You do not have long. Please be careful.

Wear your own dress and boots when you leave, so they cannot accuse you of theft.

Yours,
Briddie Hicks

~

To Mary
From Declan
April 12, 1870

Mary,

I have seen him twice and now I know that the watch is missing from his vestments. I will come by tomorrow for it. If you resist in any way, I will tell. I have read your other letter and I know the girl will write or come soon. I will keep her away by destroying her letter or by whatever means necessary if you do things my way. Expect my knock in the afternoon or evening, as soon as I am done in my vigil for this old hag. As soon as I have your payment, you will have my cooperation.

D.T.

~

Mary tossed the notes into the fire and watched the paper curl up and burn in shades of orange to blue. She could not leave as soon as Briddie had pressed her to. If she left on her own, it would take her hours upon hours to walk to Hembin, which would give her friends ample time to come up in a carriage and intercept her, for good or for evil. She had no money with her to hire a carriage or go in the public transport. Even if she did, someone would see her and testify that she got off at Hembin, which would make it easy for the authorities to search for and find her there in the town. So, leaving on her own was out of the question, and Declan couldn't take her until Friday. She had no way of knowing when Roy would have to send Agnes's letter. She just knew he was putting it off as long as possible. She feared now that the real Agnes might ruin the whole plan.

Just then, someone knocked on her door in quick succession. She wrapped a robe over her sleeping gown and answered the door to find Arthur disheveled and seemingly upset. She already knew why, but played aloof much to her pain.

"Mary, it's my pocket watch. Have you seen it? I used to wear it right here," he said, signaling. "On the sofa, when we were... *together*, I might have dislodged it."

He let himself in and looked under the sofa and behind it. He then moved the floral pillows and shook them and loosely tucked his hand between the cushion and the back of the sofa. Mary's stomach was tensed up to knots. Of course, if he found it, he would think it an accident, and she would have to steal it again. Oh, how had our sweet little diaper-changing, coffee-serving Mary Potts descended so low into trickery and seduction for gain?

The fear of prison drove her to this desperation. Oh, it was all slimy, pale Declan's fault. Well, mostly. She should never have taken the suitcase in the first place. She simply should have said no. Never should have hopped into Arthur Prickwhile's carriage or onto his ballroom dance floor. Never should have slept in his guest room bed.

"It's not here," he groaned, disappointed. "My grandfather Prickwhile gave that watch to me. He got it on a trip to America in the year 1820. That watch has traveled the entire globe. It was the only thing I had of him."

She was surprised that a person who seemingly had the whole world in terms of possessions would become upset over a sentimental timepiece. Her heart wrenched within her. "My dear Arthur, I'm very sorry."

"Yes," he muttered, looking lost, and took her hand. "If you see it, do tell me. It was very precious to me. If I did not lose it here with you, I lost it on my walk after dinner, and in order to find it I must retrace very many steps... hours' worth. That's enough. It is late. I will leave you." He must have been quite distracted by the absence of his watch because he made no physical advance toward Mary and left quietly.

―

Mary slept hard, but woke up when it was still dark with a dry throat and decided to go into the Sunshine Room where she knew a pitcher of water with glasses was set out nightly for anyone with thirst. She wore Agnes's cotton night dress and a floral robe over it with her curly hair braided to the side. The stairway and hallways were dark as she tiptoed to the Sunshine Room in her stockings and poured herself some water and drank.

The gardens which were visible through the large windows of the Sunshine Room looked altogether lovely in the moonlight. She set her glass on a table and stepped close to the windows to admire the gardens, and the rolling hills of the Mannerley countryside in the background, and off to the right, the lake. Her breath fogged up the glass.

"It is almost a full moon," said a warm, masculine voice.

She twirled around to see Mr. Singh sitting calmly on one of the floral sofas in the dark, holding a glass of brandy, still dressed in his suit, black hair swept back from his handsome, tan face. "It will be full on Good Friday. They say the full moon brings out the worst in people."

"Mr. Singh, you startled me." Mary chuckled and sat beside him, though she knew not why. Some magnetic force within him drew her to himself, as if she already knew him. As if she were somehow tethered to him. As if he weren't a cheat.

"I did not mean to. I am sitting here thinking since after dinner, and I cannot make sense of my thoughts. I worry."

His thick black lashes fluttered under a few perplexed blinks. She could see the shadow of his facial hair enveloping his cheeks and chin, around his plump mouth.

"You worry about what?" She rested her head on the back of the sofa. His presence calmed her. His voice was melodic.

"Has Arthur grieved you in some way? Has he done you wrong? Perhaps physically? Or pushed you to sensual behavior?"

"Mr. Singh, I don't know why you worry so much about my personal life. Arthur has not hurt me or grieved me. If anything, I have grieved him."

"Because you love him, and he does not want to commit?"

Mary sighed. "I am so torn. I feel the need to be honest with you. I feel as though you were drawing out the truth from deep within me, like I can't resist you."

"Well then, flow forth; speak."

"I find Arthur very attractive, and he dotes on me. I should love him, but I do not."

"You do not love him," Mr. Singh repeated as though it were the world's newest and best discovery. Then he shifted his body to see her straight on. "Mary, where do you come from?"

Port Lazáre. "Greece."

"What do you do?"

Serve food and clean. "I... socialize and travel."

"Do you know what love is? Have you ever been in love?"

If Mary had not been honest before, she was determined to be now. "From what I have seen, Mr. Singh, love always means giving up something, some sort of sacrifice. Whether it be giving up where you live, or what you have, or your expectations, in order to buy the pearl of greater value—the love of your life."

They sat in silence for a while before Mary spoke again.

"Have you come to a conclusion about the spark between us?" she asked him.

"Yes," he said, mysteriously.

"I should love to know it."

"And one day you shall," he said. "For now, let us try."

He moved closer to her, but she remained stone-still. She was already a thief and a liar; she was unwilling to become an adulteress. Three commandments in one week were far too many to break.

He held his hand straight up in the air, so innocent, with seemingly no sensual intentions. How much harm could it do to touch his rough, tan hand? Slowly, Mary lifted her hand and extended and spread her fingers, just like he was doing, telling herself that this was not *quite* adulterous. Then, they brought their hands together ever so slowly, so that their fingertips joined pair by pair and their palms rested on one another.

"I feel it," she said in wonder.

"So do I," he whispered, looking deeply into her eyes.

There were no men like him in all of England. He looked to her like a Saudi prince from a romance novel or a rugged North African voyager her mother had told her about. He was exotic, so enticing, and altogether captivating. But he was even more than that; he was her Indian military man with a doctor's training. He was her dear Mr. Singh that called to her heart and overwhelmed her, even with so little contact and so little conversation. She knew so little about him.

Still, she was being drawn further and further into this obsession. But, just then, three quick thoughts broke into her mind and interrupted the enchantment: her passionate kiss with Arthur, stealing his watch, and the thought of Mrs. Singh crying over her broken marriage.

"No," Mary said quickly, standing and removing her hand. "I must go. Good night."

She turned to leave, but was instantly stopped by Mr. Singh's warm grasp around her wrist. Just as quickly as he'd clasped around her arm with his electrifying touch, he loosened his hold, letting her hand fall again. Mary cradled her arm—in no way hurt—but rather, wanting to cherish the contact longer.

"I can't let you leave. Not like this." Mr. Singh took a step closer in the dimly lit room, studying her face with frustrated longing. They now stood facing one another, inches, yet worlds apart. "Not when there is so obviously something between us. Some sort of misunderstanding. I can't bear it any longer. You must tell me what keeps you from me, or I shall go mad."

Tears pricked Mary's eyes. "Mr. Singh," she started, her chin wobbling, "my guilt overwhelms me." Now she sobbed, and he led her back to the sofa, where they sat, his arm around her protectively.

"Please be open with me. Something is obscuring our clarity, our communication. Some awful thing is not allowing our hearts to join. We must eschew this and speak the unspoken, and unblock our souls from one another."

"Alright," Mary said, also ready to stop holding back and address things forthright, even if the answer hurt. "But, sir, the topic is uncomfortable."

"I am ready." His eyes were serious and his face concentrated.

"Though I feel you should already know this, I must tell you that I cannot and will not share you with another." Her relief was instant, and she sucked in air the way one does between fits of tears.

Mr. Singh fought back a chuckle. "Don't tell me Antoinetta has fallen for me? I am an irresistible fellow but have not been known to snag ladies who were already spoken for."

"Would you joke about a subject as serious as this?" Mary asked, annoyed. He cocked his head, obviously not understanding at all. She took a deep breath and decided to be direct. "Mr. Singh, you are an outrageous flirt, and your wife is here with us in this very home. How can you expect me to be calm when falling for you is against my religion and against my own conscience?"

"My wife?" Mr. Singh asked. His deeply concerned face froze, then turned into the widest, most genuine smile. He laughed so hard he nearly fell off the sofa, and was entirely too loud for the quiet, night setting. "So that's it!" He slapped his knee.

"What?" Mary demanded.

Advik leaned in closer to her, clasping both her hands, still reeling in his laughter. "Mary, Indira Singh is my older sister. She also married a Mr. Singh, of no relation to us."

"But that can't be," Mary protested. "You're tricking me. I asked Indira if she was married to you, and she said yes. I even asked Arthur if you and Indira were married, and he said he was at your wedding."

Mr. Singh laughed sweetly at Mary's objections. "Mary," he said amusedly, taking her hand, "trust me. I would know if I were married, and I am not. I am freer than a hawk over the moors. And *certainly* know my own sister."

"But what reason would they have to lie to me?" Mary asked, not fully trusting.

"No doubt Arthur lied to gain an advantage towards winning you for himself. But Indira? No. Her claws do come out quickly for any trivial dispute, but I suspect a misunderstanding."

"Yes, perhaps," Mary said trepidatiously, trying to recollect the details of the conversation. "In fact, now that I am concentrating on the matter, I am sure that I asked her if she was married to 'Mr. Singh.'"

"Which, she *is*," Advik said gleefully. "And to my sister, I am only, and always, Advik. *Never* Mr. Singh. That is her husband." Advik now held both of Mary's arms, innocent eyes alight.

Mary hardly knew what to do with herself. Now, the truth hit her, and pure joy flowed through her, and such freedom as she had never felt before—freedom to pursue the forbidden; freedom to love who she wanted to love. The weight was all gone off her shoulders. The moral impediment that had so frustrated her for days had been lawfully removed. She was no adulteress!

Prohibitions lifted, she raised her hands to each side of Advik's dark mane, digging her fingers into his silky, black locks. Her heart pounded hard as she combed through his hair, and he hummed melodically. Raising his hand to her own, he cradled it there on his chiseled cheek and leaned in ever so slightly toward her lips.

"So, it was nothing then?" he asked, letting a small, breathy laugh escape through his smile. "It was nothing at all."

Mary, in turn, tilted her face as if to meet a potential kiss. "My Advik. And now you can truly be mine."

Slowly, sweetly, Advik pressed his lips to Mary's.

If his touch had provoked a spark, this kiss was that dynamite thing that Mary had read about being used in a recent war. It shattered everything—all her fear, longing, frustration, and guilt. It razed it all, making all things new.

A creak and quick steps on the staircase to the foyer had Mary and Advik jumping apart. It was not appropriate for them to be together, alone in the dark, much less kissing. They shouldn't be caught in such a scandalous state.

"Probably a servant," Advik whispered, straightening his cravat and smoothing back his hair. "Go up to your room. I'll wait here for a while, so we're not seen together. We can continue this talk tomorrow. As for me, I can rest easy tonight knowing we are in good standing."

"Better than good," Mary whispered, giving his hand a squeeze.

"Goodnight, Mary," Advik said, now kissing her cheek. She parted from his embrace and flew up the stairs, her steps light and soundless.

Not encountering any servants or Mannerley guests on the stairs, she wondered for a moment who could've made the noises they'd just heard on the staircase.

That is, until she walked into her room and found Indira Singh sitting on her sofa in her night dress, holding a candle in a chamberstick. The orange glow of the small, flickering flame illuminated her somewhat menacing face.

"Mrs. Singh, I..." Mary started. "How did you get in here?"

"Your door was unlocked," Indira said, unbothered. "Let's not waste time, Mary. I saw you with my brother."

"Mrs. Singh, this was all a horrible misunderstanding. I thought you and Advik were married. Imagine my surprise when—"

"Enough!" Indira shrieked.

Mary was worried she might draw attention to the two of them, though she might have preferred to be rescued. She glanced over her shoulder into the dark hallway. Nothing there moved. She was alone with this woman and more scared than ever before.

"Let me be clear," Indira threatened. "You will stay away from Advik. You will not flirt with him or kiss him anymore."

Mary took in a quaking breath. "But why?"

"Because he's engaged."

Mary's heart started hard. She'd just gotten over the shock of him not being married, only to learn he'd pledged his heart to another. But could she trust Indira?

"To whom?"

"Beatrice Stallwood." Indira moved closer to Mary, slowly, methodically. She stood in front of her, looking up into Mary's eyes. "The half-Indian daughter of a viscount. Do you think you can compete?"

Mary tried hard to reign in her emotions. She swallowed hard. To her, and hopefully to Mr. Singh, title didn't matter over feelings. "Advik loves me, and—"

Indira laughed derisively. "Love? No, Mary. Come, now. He couldn't love a girl..." Indira looked Mary up and down. "... like *you*." Now she smiled and spoke lower. "I know exactly what you are. *Who* you are." Her smile grew wider, and Mary shivered under an eerie chill. There was no way Indira knew her real identity and profession. Declan wouldn't have told her—it would ruin his plan—and Indira wasn't there the night of the chimney soot disaster at The Drabbe. She had to be bluffing.

Unless she truly was a clairvoyant.

Mary gulped.

"Stay away from Advik, and don't mention Beatrice to him or anyone," Indira said. "Or I'll tell everyone who you are. You will finish out your week and go on your way to wherever you're from, which certainly isn't Greece." Indira's eyes narrowed in the candlelight. Her icy, free hand gripped Mary's upper arm. "I love my brother. And I won't have someone of no importance ruining his future. Do you understand?"

Mary didn't have a choice. Her true identity couldn't be exposed now; not when she'd almost made it through the ruse unscathed. The thought of a Victorian prison flashed through her mind, and then Roy and Briddie and her nieces and nephews that she loved so much. Her family.

"I understand," Mary said, and she meant it, though she could barely muster her voice to speak.

"Good," Indira said, releasing her arm and heading to the door before turning back to address Mary one last time. "Not a word," she warned, then disappeared into the dark night.

As Mary lit her lamp, trembling under sudden tears, Advik entered the room quietly, and her heart wanted her to run into his arms and tell him everything.

But she couldn't risk being unmasked by Indira, and anger smoldered in her heart towards him yet again. It is true that engagement is not marriage, but he had still given his word. Did his promise to Beatrice mean nothing to him? Could Mary love a man that so flippantly swapped women?

"Are you alright, my dove?" Advik asked, approaching Mary.

She sucked in a breath and tried to dominate her voice as she addressed him. "Advik, I've thought better of all this. I believe this is a mistake. I must ask you to leave now."

Her heart twisted at uttering these words.

In the dim lamplight, Advik's face fell. "But I thought we'd cleared the air—"

"Please, leave." She pursed her lips and lifted her chin to give herself the air of confidence that was nowhere near her at the moment.

Advik's brow furrowed in confusion. He looked so sad, so forlorn.

So handsome.

But he couldn't be hers. He was someone else's. In any other circumstance, she'd fight for him; tell him everything and hope he'd choose her over Beatrice.

But she wasn't free to do so. Too much was at stake.

"Of course," he muttered, face fallen. "I don't understand, but I won't force my presence on you, if you want me gone."

He was provoking her to take it back, to say she hadn't meant it. But then she remembered Indira's warning. She had to stand firm.

"Good night, sir," Mary said detachedly.

And Mr. Singh, looking suddenly somber, took his leave.

CHAPTER THIRTEEN

The Fifth Day—Morning

And so, dear reader, the situation grew heated on Wednesday, April 13th in the morning as the six young guests of Mannerley estate sat eating their breakfast together in the great dining room, all their heads whirring with thoughts, though they sat in near silence except for occasional, and almost unbearable, small talk.

Four of them looked as though they had come off an all-night binge of drink and dance, wincing as though their heads hurt; hearts heavy with burdens and worries, miserable to say the least. The other two were oblivious to the rest, infatuated with a newfound rush of love, but it's not the two you think. I shall allow you into their heads a bit to separate the troubled from the ecstatic.

First was stubbly and bag-eyed Arthur Prickwhile, whose hair was uncombed, cravat loosened, and a few buttons undone. He cleared his throat repeatedly with a deep grumble and ate his porridge and eggs staring vacantly into the flower vase. We can assume that his mood was, in part, due to Mary. This was the second or third time she'd made him suffer, though we know why she allowed the intimate encounter—to save her own skin from prison.

As Arthur visibly sulked, he thought surely he had done something very bad to Mary to be immediately punished by God with the loss of his precious heirloom timepiece. Perhaps he had stolen her first kiss, or scared her, or otherwise gone farther than she would have liked. He wondered within his head how many times he would find himself in this situation: offending women by being too forward, too forceful. He had attended a religious program for this issue. He thought he was better. Would there be any remedy for him?

He recalled the wake of hurt females in his past. Would he ever learn? He grabbed his beer mug and turned it up and drank it till the last drop, fighting back the tears that pushed at the reddened border of his eyes.

Now you know how Arthur felt. Back to the scene around the table.

"My word, brother, would you become drunk at breakfast?" Antoinetta asked, sitting straight, rosy cheeked, half-smiling, energetic, and playful. How annoying lovebirds can be when they don't read the room.

"Netta, I've lost my watch, and I'm very disappointed in myself. Let me drink." He ordered another from the server, who was not Declan.

Sleazy Declan sat in with Lady Huntron until noon when the shift changed. He would eat, then rest, then knock on Mary's door for the watch.

"I'm sorry to hear it," Antoinetta said, then squealed and gave a little jump, then giggled. She looked across the table slyly at Walt Corning, whose chubby, smiling face was red after having flirted with her feet under the table and startling her.

The next mind to explore is that of Mr. Advik Singh. He also seemed like he had not slept, and Mary knew he hadn't, but his look was not rough and upset like Arthur Prickwhile's. Instead, he seemed melancholy and perhaps lovesick. Like he wanted something but for some reason was not allowed to have it.

Indeed, all of his attempts toward Mary Agnes, at times nothing more than conversation, had been met with shock, rejection, and worry about what other people might think. Of course, now he knew this was because she thought he was married to Indira instead of related to her by blood. But their final conversation last night did not match up with the connection they'd felt in their clandestine rendezvous in the Sunshine Room. It just made no sense for her to rejoice that he could now be hers and minutes later send him out of her room with no further conversation.

But when he thought about it, Mary's rejection was to be expected. She herself had said that she had 'thought better of it.' After all, Advik was a man with no title, no noble family; a foreigner. He knew what fancy people said about him, about his skin color, about his lineage. There were other matters, too, certainly, but to him they were trivial. Small things from his past, bad decisions that left him intertwined or having promised things to certain people; but they were things that, nowadays, could easily be undone, perhaps by simply hiring a good lawyer, or sending the right letter.

Yes, in his mind, the only reason Mary could have had second thoughts would've been due to what people would say and think.

And Mr. Singh did not care what anyone thought about him and Mary. He certainly couldn't see why *she* cared. He was lord over his own matters, and no one else. His intentions were wholly pure, and he knew exactly what he wanted with Mary Agnes, even after only a few days. And he would find the time to lay out his argument clearly and plainly, and see if such a risk brought the fruit he desired. As for persuading her with his argument, he only had to think of when and where.

And here our evermore troubled Mary Potts sat at Arthur's side, but there was no warm hand on her leg today, or secret caresses of her stocking, and she was glad. It was expected that she should sit beside him. Everyone thought she loved him, even Mr. Singh had thought so before he asked her. Mary was sure that Arthur loved her, but he was so passion-driven, so confident in his appearance and so very rarely rejected that she had grown scornful of his advances, more so now that she knew he had lied to her about Advik being married as a way of gaining advantage in courtship. Despite the conniving nature of that manipulation, she had discovered that perhaps he was not as malevolent as she sometimes thought, but just arrogant and flawed with ambition. With each moment she was less inclined to feel the rush of lustful passion that his affections brought her. She was growing quite cold to him. She did not love him, though she had tried, when he seemed the more convenient option.

And then, swirling in her head, was the thought of the awful thing she had done to him. Two things really. The first was making him think he had scared or hurt her, which was not the case. Now, she worried about having created in him, by the second evil act of stealing his watch, the psychological dishevelment that she now observed as he listlessly lifted each strip of bacon to his mouth, staring a hole through the vase as if he had nothing and no one to live for. It is quite depressing, dear reader, to see the rich and handsome so dreadfully pouty.

This second thing she had done to him was surprisingly hurtful to him. She figured he wouldn't miss the watch, which had been part of her justification for doing it. But the absence of the timepiece was absolutely eating him up.

Then came her own fears: Agnes's letter, and having to trust awful Declan for more than one thing, his protection and surveillance of any incoming letters, and later his help in her escape. Her future was in his hands, even her life. Her escape and her hiding at The Drabbe would not be easy. They might send policemen to search local establishments and arrest her. The risk was great. Death in prison was a factor in this awful lying game she was now involved in. How had she tangled herself up in this mess? She hoped that the real Agnes would not file any charges against her if she were found out. She hoped against hope that Agnes happened to be so very good.

Though she sat beside sad and now drunk Arthur, she frequently met Mr. Singh's lovesick eyes. How he longed for her in the way he looked at her.

"You're not eating much," he commented softly to Mary.

"Indeed, I'm not very hungry." Their gazes locked for a while. The corners of his plush lips turned up, producing a soft, sweet smile. She saw something in his eyes. Was it hope? Antoinetta interrupted the moment.

"Why ever not, Mary Agnes? The food is delicious!"

She was all too loud and much too happy. Mary ignored the question, shooting a quick smile her way. Walt rescued the silence by talking about his sister's encyclopedia collection which included entries on the cuisine of Germany, a subject which no one was listening to, not even Antoinetta.

Now, Mary understood how Walt could have become a man of the law; he was possessed of total recall, regardless of the importance of the fact that was drudged up, or the lack of interest of the person listening to his recitation. He always seemed correct in the smallest details of the information he regurgitated, yet any social nuance flew well above his head. As with most people, one gift's cup was full to the brim, and the other bone-dry. How the Lord varied as he poured.

Mary Potts wanted to take Mr. Singh's hand and walk off with him, away from all these people and all these problems. He was calming; he was safe.

But he was forbidden; pledged to another.

Mary glanced at Indira Singh, who sat next to Advik and across from Arthur with a tired and angry look about her. She looked coldly at Mr. Singh as he continued to gaze longingly at Mary. Indira slowly took hold of her fork, and Mary would not have been surprised if she had stabbed the back of his hand violently in a fit of sisterly rage, or out of jealousy on Beatrice Stallwood's behalf.

But she did not.

She merely gathered some eggs and ate. Just as Mary thought these things, Indira Singh's almond eyes with lashes like jet black fronds set on Mary, who wondered if she could be reading her thoughts. They did not talk; they just looked at one another. Mary was no longer scared of this small, intimidating woman, because despite what Indira perceived about Mary's deceptiveness, she would also know from her sixth sense that Mary was wholly submitted to Indira's threat.

She wouldn't mention Beatrice, she would give up her pining over Advik, and she would go back where she came from after her stay was complete. And knowing that Mary was cooperating in this way might be why a small, subtle smile formed on her lips, though her brow remained folded and serious.

Then stood Walt Corning among them, dinging his knife on his water glass much too loudly. "I have an announcement. All ears please! Everyone look here!"

Of course, they had all been looking at him from the first ding.

"Antoinetta Prickwhile and I are engaged to be married."

Antoinetta stood, beaming, at Walt's side and the two held hands and looked at their four run-down and trouble-laden friends who stared back at them blankly. The silence went on far too long.

"C-Congratulations," Mary stuttered, less enthusiastic than she intended.

"You've been together for almost a decade; this means nothing," Arthur Prickwhile grumbled. Antoinetta gasped in anger. He threw his napkin on the table and stumbled out of the dining room toward the stairs, stating he would be in his room if anyone needed him.

Mr. and Mrs. Singh looked at each other. Mrs. Singh tried to rectify it by saying he probably meant that he had been waiting for this good news for a long time.

"It is a... nice... piece of news," Mr. Singh said dryly and perhaps a bit enviously.

"What is *wrong* with you all?" Antoinetta's eyes moistened and her face turned splotchy. "My friends, at *my* table, and no one can congratulate me in earnest for my engagement? And I am even criticized?"

Mary Potts tried to smooth things over. "Antoinetta, it's not that. None of us are well today. We are all troubled for different reasons."

The negative mood of the room had finally reached Antoinetta, who gathered her things and stormed out and up the stairs, sobbing as she went.

Walt Corning, Mary Potts, and Mr. and Mrs. Singh looked around at one another. Walt Corning's mouth was round and concerned. "What a strange reaction to engagement news," he remarked simply. "I had thought us a very handsome couple."

Mary took her leave.

~

After an hour or so being unable to relax in the guestroom, Mary Potts put on her own boots and casual dress that she wore on her days off and set out to walk the gardens of Mannerley despite the gray and threatening clouds that swirled above her head. This was around eleven in the morning. She strolled through the gardens alone, talking inside her head, either to herself, or God, or Briddie. She was not sure.

She spotted a hawk gliding through the clouded sky so free, so smooth. She longed for that freedom, and considered that getting farther from Mannerley would help clear her tangled-up mind. So, she approached the gate that led out to the countryside and the lake, and she walked through it, and kept on walking. She walked so far that soon she was among hills and trees and could no longer see the house. She was not scared, as she remembered the direction she had come from. She took a rest on a large rock under an oak, watching the long grass sway with the breeze of the mounting tempest, and listening to the distant thunder roll.

She knew not why, as she was not typically a crier, but the tears fell. Now things were becoming clear. She knew what she had done to Arthur Prickwhile was horrible, and she was unsure if she could go through with it. Could she actually hand that watch over to Declan's grubby, greedy hands? Could she be so easily extorted? What happened to Mary with her will of iron? Mary with her upright and confident nature? The Mary that was like Briddie and Roy?

How disappointed they would be in her was her next thought. And this surely provoked the tears. She sobbed hard and hugged her knees, not even sure who she was anymore. But she had to go through with it, or else.

A gloved hand brushed away the tangle of curls that enveloped her tragic episode. She lifted her streaming face. It was glowing Mr. Singh. He had walked up quietly leading his horse.

"Why do you cry, Mary Agnes?" he asked.

But she did not answer. He sat beside her, very close. His arm caught her torso and leaned her on himself, as if it were the most natural thing in the entire world. Her whole body tingled, and she was sure his did, too. His breathing was excited, warm, manly. She looked up into his deep brown eyes that communicated such peace, such safety. Oh, how she loved Mr. Singh. How she wished he was not already taken. How she wished she had no need to submit to controlling older sisters.

For now, where no one could see, she sank into him and received his comfort, breaking part of her oath to Indira in a moment of fleshly weakness.

"Mr. Singh," she said, sniffling and resolving to speak in riddles about Arthur and his watch, "I am very close to my sister. She had a horse she loved very much, but I had to sell that horse from under her as I am in charge of those kinds of things at our estate, and I would have fallen into a great debt had I not sold it. The amount of this debt, when paired with others, could have sent me to jail. But my sister, who loves me, will be heartbroken. But I cannot do as she wants because I must look out for myself. And the sale of the horse has been in large part a secret from her. Do you see my predicament?"

Mr. Singh thought about it. "Yes, yes, I do."

Then, Mary spoke about Mr. Singh and the forbidden topic of Beatrice in a similarly riddled way. "Separately, and adding to my discontentment, I have two workers. One of them is good and nice. I believe he would do a good enough job on the estate. But the other is the one I prefer—now he can *really* work. It has come to my attention that he is already hired elsewhere, and I will have to let him go and not have him on the estate anymore. This saddens me because I feel like he is the best worker I have ever known, and I do not want to part from him. But it cannot be that he works for two people at one time. It is not fair to the one who hired him first, though I long to have him for myself."

"I see," Mr. Singh said.

"So, I am battering myself for what I have done to my sister, and longing for things to be different with my workers."

"May I advise you, or do you only want to be heard?"

Mary smiled. How pleasant for a man to ask such a thing. "Please, guide me in these matters."

"Very well. Your sister, if she loves you, must understand what you have done. I do not think it noble that you have taken about selling the horse in secret; that will be the hurtful part of it. Had you simply asked your sister, she may have come up with some other way of financing the thing. You have acted poorly, but what is done is done. You should collect the sum and explain it. Perhaps she will forgive you. Jail for a woman is no small thing, and the prisons in England are very cruel. I do not blame you at all for desiring to avoid that. It is very much understandable when framed that way.

"About your workers, it is more complicated. It is as you have said, if the best worker is already hired, it's just too bad. You will have to get along with the one available to you, or else rid yourself of him too and hope someone better comes along," Mr. Singh said, unaware he was talking about himself, Arthur, and Beatrice. "Or have you thought of talking directly with the place where he works? Perhaps those who hired him would be willing to let him go if you're so decided upon having him."

Mary shook her head slowly and sadly. "No, Mr. Singh. That certainly cannot be done. A contract made is something I would never try to disrupt. And I have doubly made sure that the contract is indeed valid. I have no other recourse but to forget about him." Mary Potts said all this while cradled in his arm against his beating heart. Again, it hit her that he was not hers at all, and never could be, when he was promised to another. She did not know why she entertained fantasies of him, why she let him hold her in this way; what did she hope would come of them?

The only road leading from her thoughts about Mr. Singh was a treacherous one, consisting of either her being exposed as a barmaid, or poor, betrothed Beatrice being heartbroken. Other than this fledgling breed of romance—holding each other in secret—there was no other relational option with Mr. Singh, for mere friendship would not satisfy, and would even be more painful.

First a touch of the hand and a kiss in the Sunshine Room alone after dark. Now an embrace against his chest alone in the countryside. What would be next?

Of course, he had already kissed her hand in the courtyard of The Drabbe days before. And to his knowledge, that girl was a completely different person. The man seemingly had no restraint. His spirit emitted pure trustworthiness and comfort, but his actions showed otherwise. He was willing to entertain flirtations and small physical advances with a variety of women in private, despite his promise. Of what value, then, was his word? No matter how much Mary was drawn to him, she would never want a man to do that to her.

Still, she enjoyed the moment while it lasted. Though she knew after it was over, she would need to put distance between them, in order to come through this Mannerley ordeal as emotionally unscathed as possible—if that were even still an option. Distance, because she knew it was best, but it was also what she had sworn to Indira—or else.

"Come, now," he said, standing and extending his hand to her. He helped her mount sidesaddle on the horse and then led her toward Mannerley as the raindrops from the approaching storm came stronger and faster. "You know," he called back to her, handing her his coat without looking upon her wet and clingy clothes, "I like the way you look today; simple dress, comfortable boots. I believe you are in your own skin. And you are just as lovely as ever."

She suddenly realized as she put on his coat during this encounter with Advik Singh, though she had spoken in riddles, everything she had said was true to her, even down to her clothing and shoes. "Thank you, sir," she said, "for everything."

Mr. Singh offered to let Mary off near the garden, but she declined, saying she would rather go with him to leave the horse in the stable and walk back together even in the rain. Her nervousness about soon meeting Declan made her not want to be alone. So, that is precisely what they did, except they ran instead of walked to the front doors of Mannerley because the rain picked up to a steady pour. Mr. Singh was absolutely soaked. Mary's curls were weighed down and dripping. She wore his coat that hung large and limp on her much smaller frame.

When they got inside the front doors, laughing and exhilarated as they were, they drip-dried in the entryway, and Mary handed him back his coat. She did not care if she was immodest. Being with Mr. Singh was like being in front of a mirror anyway; he understood her, and he valued her. There was no hiding her true heart from him. Time froze as they smiled into each other's eyes.

"Advik, you must dry off at once, and then we must have a conversation."

The sharp remark came from Mrs. Singh, who stood atop the grand staircase glowering at them, dressed in a blood-red saree with gold embroidery. The color made her skin absolutely glow. Mary was taken aback by her beauty and suddenly sensed that she was very inferior to Indira in her own flimsy cotton dress and old boots.

"Yes, yes, Indira. At once. Mary Agnes," he said and gave a slight bow, running up the stairs to Mrs. Singh. Mary's heart fell.

Instead of following Advik to talk, Indira calmly stared down at Mary as he disappeared into the hall.

"Our agreement, Mary Agnes?" she asked in a low voice, just loud enough for Mary to hear.

"I-it still stands," Mary stuttered, nervous to the core. "I didn't mention anything. He's just accompanied me home due to the heavy rains."

Indira stared at Mary, presumably reading her, perhaps deciphering if she were telling the truth.

"You have my word," Mary said, trying again. Her tone was pleading, and it sickened her.

"Good," Indira said, satisfied. She turned and followed where Advik had gone.

Mary exhaled hard, clutching her chest. Right at that moment, the clock struck one, and she remembered it was the afternoon. Declan.

Mary focused on the task at hand. She needed to stop all contact with Mr. Singh at once. It was all too painful, and it would lead to absolutely nothing good. She never wanted to feel like she just had with Indira again. With Declan about to collect the watch, the heist was almost done. She could be out of this place in no time, and back to her life in Hembin.

Now she needed to go to her room, change her clothes, and wait for Declan's knock. She would give him what he wanted, and she would do it quickly. And after getting this great sin over with, she would try to do everything else from there on out righteously. It should be the only dark spot on her recent record. May God forgive her.

CHAPTER FOURTEEN

Agnes's Letter

Had there ever been such a kind, dedicated and multi-talented worker at The Drabbe as Agnes? The tall blonde thing fell immediately into favor with everyone, earned generous tips, and worked hard. The children loved her very much, and Roy and Briddie had been lucky that one of them had not spoken too much of where Aunt Mary was, exactly, and about the gold-lettered traveling trunk that they had all undoubtedly seen. Agnes had become sincerely inspired by working there and had now begun throwing around ideas about starting her own restaurant and inn, though with nicer rooms to attract fancier guests.

It was true that her parents had wonderful connections, fancy friends, and plenty of money to live comfortably, but she was no Antoinetta Prickwhile. She did not have a family business that produced great wealth to be handed down to her. She would have to choose some sort of profession and work hard to maintain her comfort and lifestyle and ensure that her future children would also have prosperity. It was so easy to sink into poverty in Victorian England. All she would need for success was the initial investment in property and furniture, perhaps from her father.

Halfway through her workweek, on Wednesday, at the exact same time that Mary Potts was taking her walk in the countryside and was comforted by Mr. Singh, Agnes found herself in the kitchen after wiping the tables, preparing for the upcoming lunch service. Roy was at her side, and they spoke of proprietorship and cleanliness standards, shipments of goods, and anything else she would need to know if she became serious about the business. Roy was a wealth of knowledge, and she was thankful for him, and sad her week would soon end. It was during this conversation and these feelings that she saw the small white corner of a paper envelope jutting out from Roy's interior jacket pocket.

"Oh, what's this?" she asked him.

He looked at it, and his face grew unusually pale. "I... don't know."

"Well, pull it out, then," Agnes pressed him. She knew she could be nosey and frequently drove others crazy with her attention to detail and inquisitiveness. It would do her well as a businesswoman.

Roy retrieved the envelope slowly, but was he sweating? Was he nervous? He spoke: "Unfortunately, Agnes... it seems to be your letter. The one you wrote to Lady Huntron."

"Oh, no! It was never sent!" Agnes grew frantic; she had longed to fix this situation as soon as possible, and now she would have to wait even longer.

"I am sorry," Roy said.

Agnes pulled herself together and showed him grace.

"No, Roy. Don't feel badly. It simply slipped your mind. I know you are very busy here, and I do not blame you. Forgetfulness happens to everyone. Hand me the letter, and I will go now before lunch service and put it in the post myself."

"Thank you for understanding." Roy handed Agnes her letter, ever so slowly. When she clasped it, Roy held it just as strong between his forefinger and thumb. Agnes had to give it a little wiggle and jerk to free it from his grasp. Plastered on his face was a wide-eyed, nervous pout.

Odd.

Perhaps he had delayed it on purpose, not wanting such a great worker to leave.

She burst into a breathy smile to reduce the uncomfortableness of the moment, and jetting across the street, she had it sent.

CHAPTER FIFTEEN

The Fifth Afternoon—Afternoon

Mary had rushed upstairs and taken the watch from its place under the sofa cushions and nervously put it under her bed pillow. She knew what she had to do and dreaded it. She needed Declan's silence and his help for her escape. She prayed the real Agnes would hold off writing or visiting for two more days. By Friday midday, Mary Agnes Riboneaux would vanish like the phantom she was.

She hung her wet clothing near the fire to dry, but noticed it was dying down. She threw on another log and prodded at it with the great iron stoker, leaving it in the flame carelessly as she put on her chemise and Agnes's floral robe. The clock had struck two not long before. And suddenly there came a knock. She knew exactly who it was and what he was there for. Her anxious stomach dripped with dread and her whole belly was in knots. Her hands started to shake, and she walked over to the door and spoke through it sternly to slimy, heartless Declan Thobbs before letting him in.

"I know what you are here for. I have suffered the past days like never before by your doing. But I need you, so I will do it. I will pay the price. I will give it to you, and I will give it freely, if only to be done with this awful tension between us. Now come in and take what is yours."

Mary slung open the door and to her great surprise Arthur Prickwhile, with a devilishly impassioned look in his eye, pounced on her, kicking the door closed and pressing his lips to hers. He overpowered her severely, ultimately pushing her onto the plush rug in front of the hearth, from which place she could not escape as his heavy, muscular body was now on top of hers.

"I came to apologize," he said between fervent kissing, undoing her robe. "What better way than this. How glad I am to have your consent!"

"Arthur, no!" Mary called out, struggling against the act.

"Are you in earnest?" he asked near her ear, quite confused, while untucking his shirt and starting on his belt. "You practically begged me for this and now you would have me to stop?" Roughly, he pulled up her chemise.

"No, Arthur, stop at once!" Mary panicked.

"Are you *truly* in earnest?" Arthur spoke with great compassion and hesitated just a split-second, and he really may have stopped altogether, but Mary would never know as right at that moment that he mouthed the question, she struck the back of his calves with the red-hot fire poker, singeing through his garments and deeply burning his lower legs.

He screamed loudly. A worried Antoinetta ran in not long after with Declan behind her, glowering but enjoying the scene. Mary Potts was now shaking and in tears from her place under Arthur Prickwhile, who was lifting himself up and making himself decent. She had never felt power like he had, sheer strength. And now she cried from embarrassment at what the intruders were seeing.

"Not again! I thought you were reformed!" Antoinetta shouted at her brother and scrambled to Mary's side as Arthur backed away, hobbling, and talking to Mary as he went.

"What else could you have meant when you spoke through the door?"

To her surprise his eyes filled with hurt and angry tears.

"Or, did you think you spoke to another man? Yes, that's it. The message wasn't for me. One of the dozens of workers here, perhaps? How little I knew you, Mary Agnes. How very little I knew you. I thought you pure and delighted in undoing your purity myself. But you are a flower visited by many bees before."

Mary's face grew red in anger and hot tears dropped from her eyes. Would he attack her, and then accuse her?

"Leave at once," Mary ordered Arthur with the tight throat and gravelly voice that come with fury.

"This place will be mine, and you would order me to leave?" Arthur asked arrogantly, obviously angry.

Declan still stood at the door taking in every dramatic detail as one watches a spontaneous street fight. Antoinetta fumed at Mary's side, and it was she who defended Mary.

"This place will also be mine. Go to your bed chamber, brother. Leave this woman alone. Do not blame her, for I know this has been a pattern for you."

Arthur looked back and forth between the two of them. "Indeed, I must go. The burns are deep and searing. I am in great pain and will require a nurse and bandages, no doubt. It is difficult even to stand."

"I shall arrange for your care, Mr. Prickwhile," Declan said from the doorway.

"Yes," Arthur said to Declan, and then added, "and you saw nothing. None of your work mates need know of this. I know how you lower class feed on the drama of us dandies. You will keep it a secret. Or you will be without a job, forever."

"Yes, sir." Declan nodded from his place by the door, and Arthur hobbled out.

"Oh, Mary," Antoinetta moaned and held her wilted friend in her arms. "Come to bed. I will go at once and make some tea. Your spirits will be brightened by it. Don't fret over this. Please don't fret." Antoinetta covered Mary with her blankets and gave her a handkerchief to blot her tears. She sat on her bed briefly and rubbed the curls out of her face. She kissed her forehead softly. "I will be right back." She walked quickly out of the room, probably assuming Declan would keep a protective, stoic watch.

Declan, however, smiled malignantly upon her exit.

Now, Mary did not mind doing what she knew she had to do. She hated Arthur for accusing her of being promiscuous. She hated him for the way he pressed his body onto hers, the way he subdued her with unmatched strength. She shuddered at what might have happened. He said he loved her, but love was not supposed to be that way. Mr. Singh would *never* act that way.

Being as she and Declan were alone, she drew out the watch from under her pillow and handed it to him. The gold chain slinked into his clammy hand. Neither spoke. He tucked the timepiece in his own breast pocket and went his way.

And after tea and a few brief words with Antoinetta, Mary stayed in bed till the next morning.

CHAPTER SIXTEEN
Lady Huntron's Pile of Correspondence

You remember, of course, Agnes Ann Riboneaux's letter to Lady Huntron. It is of this matter that I, Rutherford Wells, now speak.

How unfortunate a time for poor Declan to be sorting the mail and trying to guard against Agnes's correspondence. He hopped around busy all the time anyway, and he very much loathed any effort at work. Then added to this stress was alternating care for Lady Huntron, who was somewhat better on Mary Potts's sixth day at Mannerley, which was Thursday, April 14, and she had even risen for an early breakfast and a short walk before retiring again to her bed, but more on that later.

I mention that it was an unfortunate time for Declan because, not only was he busy and in charge of mail service, but it also became popular around that time for the well-off younger folks to send Easter greeting cards to anyone and everyone they knew of similar or higher rank. And Lady Huntron, who always doted on the youth, was very popular among the age group who sent these cards. So, during Holy Week in 1870, as is imaginable, hundreds of these Easter images poured in, some with Christ crucified or Christ risen, others with eggs, bunnies, children, flowers. And one very odd card featured Humpty Dumpty. What *he* had to do with Easter, Declan had no idea.

The problem with these cards is that many times they were sent bare, but other times they were sent in envelopes just like a normal letter. At first Declan tried to sort the mail as soon as it came into Lady Huntron's chamber, searching for any possible letter from Agnes specifically in order to burn it. If Mary were caught lying and charges were pressed against her, honest Mary would probably rat Declan out, and then he'd be in jail right along with her. He needed to escape on Good Friday. He needed to sell the watch and make a name for himself in Port Lazáre. He needed to intercept any letter from Agnes, though he knew not if one would come.

Declan could not keep up this everyday-sorting-business very long because on Wednesday, when Arthur was injured, Declan had another rich whiny baby to take care of instead of just old Huntron, so he could not dedicate time to it. By Thursday, Mary's sixth day, the cards and letters accumulated in a formidable pile. He fingered through them loosely as the breakfast bell rang. Time for food and tea service again.

He groaned. Oh, he was so sick of working. If he had his way he would never, ever work again. He quickly told the girl taking over his shift to leave the correspondence as it was; he would get to it later. She said alright, and out he went, but of course he did not see the girl forget his instructions completely, and lay all the cards and letters on the tea table next to Lady Huntron's bedside, just as the old woman came in from her early morning breakfast and walk.

The girl helped Lady Huntron into bed after changing her clothes and propped her up on some pillows.

"My, what a mountain of letters," Lady Huntron remarked. "Have I been so sick? I must start chipping away at them. Hand me a few, every hour or so, so I may make some progress."

"Yes, ma'am," the girl servant said and handed her four or five of the cards and letters, not paying attention to which she gave her.

Lady Huntron read, as she would off and on all day and evening, between rests.

And at the very bottom of the correspondence pile was a white envelope, a bit grimy from being stored in a working man's jacket, with the return address of The Drabbe Inn and Pub, and the name Agnes Ann Riboneaux in the top left corner.

It was only a matter of time until sick old Lady Huntron learned the truth.

CHAPTER SEVENTEEN

The Sixth Day

On Thursday morning, another tense breakfast was taking place, but this time in the Sunshine Room, and the only aloof one who did not perceive the awkwardness was chubby Walt Corning.

Mary sipped her tea and did not part her eyes from the cup. There was nowhere to look, for she could not have Mr. Singh as she had decided to give him up and thus could not dart her eyes his way for fear of communicating continuance. She could not look at Antoinetta for fear of bursting into tears.

Arthur was in his room with the excuse of nursing a horse-riding injury, and he was who she usually looked at just because she was normally paired with him. If she glanced at Walt, he would start some insufferable small-talk, and she certainly did not want to see Mrs. Indira Singh ever again. Her tea was quite interesting anyway. It distorted her face into unfathomable features; perhaps it was a reflection of her deceitful spirit, all twisted up and contorted.

"I've just seen Lady Huntron go upstairs to rest. I was glad to see her up and walking again. You know, when the elderly get sick, they sometimes die," Walt Corning said, chewing loudly and slurping his tea.

No one responded, so Mr. Singh spoke up and took an arrow for the army. "Yes, I have heard that is common," he mumbled, emotionless.

"Antoinetta, dear," Walt Corning tried again after too much silence, "won't you tell your lady friends of our wedding plans?"

She finished chewing her food, motioning for the rest to wait. Then politely but reluctantly informed everyone that they would be married in summer at the estate. She would be settling in England and would only return to India if needed. Arthur and the aides she had trained would maintain her part of the business. She would still have an income from it, but she would be focusing on her marriage and learning to handle Mannerley's upkeep while Lady Huntron was still alive.

"I will certainly miss you. You are a true friend. A toast," Indira Singh said and lifted her teacup.

"A toast with tea, Indira?" Mr. Singh asked critically.

Evidently, whatever they'd talked about after the rainstorm had stirred up some old tension.

"Yes, Advik. A toast with tea." Indira's voice seethed contempt.

Everyone, even Mary, had to raise his cup to chink everyone else's, and she quickly did a survey of everyone's faces she had been avoiding. Walt's rosy-cheeked smile was wide and toothy. Antoinetta's eyes were glazed over and cold. Mrs. Singh looked downright angry. But Mr. Singh, in his confident handsomeness, black hair swept back and broad shoulders, was the picture of elegant peace. She didn't want to, but her eyes met his, and she could not help but smile, ever so softly.

"Is everyone quite finished?" Mr. Advik Singh asked, and they all looked at each other nodding, but confused by the question. "Good," and then to a server, "Would you be so kind as to clear this? Thank you."

The table was cleaned, and Advik Singh stood. "I would like to speak to Mary Agnes alone." Now Mary's gaze darted up sharply. Antoinetta's brow rose with excitement, and she bit her bottom lip in anticipation.

"Why?" Walt Corning asked bluntly and a bit too loudly.

"Never mind, dear. Come along."

Antoinetta rushed off with Walt. Mary's heart pounded. What could Singh want to say?

Indira Singh pursed her lips and seared through Advik with her eyes, hotter than any fire poker in all of England. She rose quickly and stormed off. It was remarkable that such a grand stomp came from such a little woman.

But Mr. Advik Singh ignored her petulance, apparently having his mind already made up. He dismissed the servants and closed the glass doors of the Sunshine Room so he and Mary were entirely alone, then he circled around and sat beside her on the sofa, taking her hand.

"The energy we now feel," he said as their hands positively throbbed together, "is a blessing from God. I would like to feel it forever."

"Mr. Singh, I don't think I understand," Mary said meekly, exhausted from all the happenings and emotionally drained.

"I want to move to England," Mr. Singh said.

To Mary's surprise, he slid onto the plush, floral rugs in front of her, perched on only one knee. He took her left hand in his, lightly touching her dainty ring finger.

"I want you to marry me when I do."

Mary shot to her feet, hovering over him in his humble position.

"How can you say this type of thing to me?" Mary demanded, cheeks flushed, and pulled her hand free from his.

"Whatever do you mean? Is it because you love Arthur after all?"

"No, no!" Mary hid her face in her hand.

"I am sure you could grow to love me with time and—"

"Mr. Singh, I *already* love you!" After Mary spoke the words, an excited silence filled the air. Mr. Singh rose and stood directly in front of her, looking slightly down at her face as he was taller, and took both of her hands in his.

"Then what is the problem, my dear?"

His eyes implored her, searched her. He panted out his breath and held her hands tight. Her heart broke again as it had so many times. As much as she loved him, she would have to do without him. No truly moral person would so flippantly put away one fiancée to obtain another, and without the smallest hint of remorse.

"The problem is more than obvious, though you attempt to obscure it. I will not marry you, Mr. Singh. I think you very, very cruel for teasing me in this way, for asking me to do this horribly unjust thing."

"Unjust?" Mr. Singh scoffed, now a bit outraged. "A single man and a single woman—"

"Single?" quipped Mary. "Is Beatrice Stallwood now nothing to you?"

The look on Mr. Singh's face was pure shock and torture. Mary looked over her shoulder; she was sure she'd find Indira lurking there, having heard her break her promise and mention the forbidden topic of Beatrice. She was relieved when she noticed no one outside the closed, glass doors.

And mentioning his engagement, which had weighed so heavily on her chest for so long, was an immense relief. It was almost worth being exposed as a fraud, so good it felt.

She turned back to Mr. Singh, whose slight frown and forehead crease betrayed his vexation.

"Your sister told me," Mary said, dropping her voice from the accusatory tone she'd just used, "and she made me swear not to talk about it, but I can no longer stand not to."

"No, no," Advik said, now rubbing his suddenly tired face. "I'm glad the truth is out, it's only—"

"So, you admit it? It's true?"

Advik sighed heartily. "Yes and no."

"What do you mean? Speak clearly."

"It is not my engagement," Advik lamented, eyes sadder than she'd ever seen them. "It is my sister's engagement... *for me*."

Mary covered her face with her hands, ready to run up to her chambers and indulge in a good cry. But Advik went on.

"When Indira and I last spoke, after our horse ride in the rain, I told her my plans to propose to you as soon as possible, and that I had no intention of marrying Bea. She was outraged, and told me I was throwing away my chance at a connection to nobility. Beatrice is her closest friend, and it's always been an idea in her mind that she and I... and I and she... I didn't know that you knew." Advik's forlorn, lost look almost persuaded Mary to forgive him. "These kinds of things are kept secret, you see, being as I am a foreigner. Intermarriage... it's a new concept. Though the young lady has some Indian blood, she does not look it with green eyes and copper hair."

A tear escaped each of Mary's eyes, trailing down her cheeks and dripping down before her. "Your sister can never know we spoke of this. I don't know how, but she knows things about me. Things I don't want anyone to know." Mary was so close to the truth; skirting around it. If revealing a few things now to Advik felt so good, would coming clean completely truly free her conflicted spirit?

Then she remembered the stakes and thought better of it.

Advik's breath caught. "Has she threatened you?"

Mary shook her head, chin quivering. "It doesn't matter, Advik. You are someone else's betrothed. That, right now, is all that matters."

Mary turned, leaving him there in his suffering and ran, ran, ran up the stairs and into her guest chamber where she hastily packed Agnes's things just as she had originally found them. In her hurried activity, and sobbing heavily as she was, she failed to realize that Antoinetta Prickwhile had entered the room and stood behind her, shocked at the scene.

"I swear, I thought Mr. Singh was prone to propose!" Antoinetta then saw what she was occupied with. "Oh Mary Agnes, don't leave. Where would you go?"

Antoinetta tried to grab Mary's arm, but she pulled away and kept packing. "I know a place in Hembin. It's called The Drabbe. I'll walk there."

"Mary Agnes, it's a six hour walk to Hembin, and it's dangerous. You could meet any sort of thief or con man along the road."

Mary Potts laughed aloud at this and looked at Antoinetta through her tears. *A thief or a con, like myself,* she wanted to say.

"Why do you look at me that way?" Antoinetta asked. "Have I not always been a kind and good friend to you, even defending you against my own flesh and blood? Would you shun me in this way, to walk away because of my over-excited brother?"

Mary realized that Antoinetta had no idea that she loved Mr. Singh and still thought this whole thing was about Arthur.

It occurred to her suddenly that if she left now Arthur may suspect she stole his watch and made off with it. Of course, he would suspect this no matter what day it was, but if she left now, she'd have no means of transport to Hembin but walking. This would give Arthur ample time to send authorities to intercept her along the road. But if she left on Friday as planned, they'd all be distracted at church, and Declan's arranged carriage would be a faster escape.

She simply could not leave earlier. She had no means. She had to wait for Declan's plan to unfold.

She pulled herself together, dried her tears, and steered her mood in an entirely different direction: gratitude. And this time she was being honest. Antoinetta was the sweetest person in the whole, large Mannerley estate, and the one who most cared for her, because if Mr. Singh truly cared for her, he would not have asked her to do something so cruel and wrong. Her love for her friend rushed upon her.

"Yes, Antoinetta, forgive me. You have been the best kind of friend. I have enjoyed myself greatly in your home, at your expense. I do not take it lightly. Please know this week has been one of the finest in my life in terms of cuisine and accommodation. It has also been a very trying week for me. At times I have been sure that everyone around me, except for you, has lost their mind."

Antoinetta chuckled just a few times. "What are the rich to do in their abundant free time but go a little mad?"

Mary laughed with her friend, rose from where she had been frenzied with sudden organization, and hugged Antoinetta who planted a friendly kiss on her cheek. She would stick it out; she would stay. And tomorrow, Good Friday, Declan and she would make their escape, and vanish into oblivion.

CHAPTER EIGHTEEN

The Sixth Day—Night

Mary Potts spent the day in her room, somewhat fearful of encountering either Declan or Arthur in the halls of Mannerley. When she grew restless, as the day had been a very sunny one and she longed for fresh air, she tiptoed to the hallway outside of Arthur's room, where she stood by the door which was ajar and craned her neck to hear if he was in there.

Sure enough, he was having his bandages changed, and she even overheard Declan's voice as one of the servants who was over Arthur's care. She stayed a few moments by the door and overheard that Declan would soon be going to Lady Huntron's room in the west wing to sit with her for the night. Arthur asked him if he might clean up a spill that had occurred in the bath chamber when he had attempted to hobble there on his own when no one was present.

Hearing that neither of them had any plans to be out of doors, Mary Potts resolved to take a garden walk in the evening penumbra, as it was eight o'clock and the sun had just begun to set. She flitted quickly and silently down the dim hallway, down the stairs, through the Sunshine Room, and out the great glass doors, vanishing into the rows of rose bushes and privacy hedges. Here, she could breathe and be alone with her thoughts. Here she would be safe.

"Mary," called a soft, feminine voice that she did not recognize.

She turned on her heels and saw the elegant, petite Mrs. Indira Singh, her face docile like she had never seen it before.

"I was sitting on the wicker chair sorting out my own thoughts when you rushed by. I thought we might walk together."

To Mary's surprise, Indira hooked her arm to Mary's. She had no choice now. Together they started down a dark row, and silently they walked. They had given one complete turn around the moonlit garden in complete quietness, when Mary took courage.

"Does walking near me and holding my arm in this way allow you to better read my thoughts?"

Indira laughed through her nose. "I wish," she said and paused, then sighed. "No, Mary. I cannot read your thoughts. I can only discern your spirit. I see your deceit, though I do not know what it is."

"And do you know what occurred this morning in the Sunshine Room, when Mr. Singh asked you all to leave?" Now our Mary Potts became nervous.

"Yes," Indira affirmed slowly, "Yes, I do. My Advik, so guided by romance…"

After she said that, she tsked several times with her tongue, an endearing trait she must have picked up from Antoinetta.

"I do not understand this dysfunction, Mrs. Singh," Mary complained. "You attempt to control the man as if he were a twelve-year-old boy. Procuring an arranged engagement for a woman he has no interest in, and quelling, thus, the natural spark that he and I feel for one another. Surely, you who see all things, can see that Advik and I have something quite special."

To Mary's surprise, Indira smiled. "I said I see your deceitfulness, and even though this frustrates me, and I so wish you were an honest creature, I also see your good heart. I see the truthful things you have told myself and others. I see your care for Antoinetta, your kindness to the staff, your attention to and appreciation for Advik."

"So, does this mean you are no longer angry?" Mary asked, hopeful.

Indira laughed under her breath. "Indeed, at first I was angry. You may have noticed it this morning when I left breakfast. How could you have missed it, really. But now... I've accepted things. Fate has spoken, and I can no longer fight it."

Though Indira was cryptic, Mary felt as though she was giving her a blessing to love Advik, and hope swelled within her heart.

"You speak as if you will let me love your brother, after all. What would you have me do?"

At this, they stopped, and Indira faced Mary, placing her hands on her upper arms and looking firmly into her eyes. "When a man and a woman are in love, things always become complicated one way or another. But I will tell you exactly what I would have you do. You must follow your heart and do exactly what it wants. And I will get out of your way, and out of Advik's way. Yes, I will shrink back and stop being an encumbrance." Indira hooked her arm again through Mary's and led them slowly onward, along a row of shrubs.

"But will you expose me?" Mary asked, still somewhat fearful.

"Mary, I have nothing to expose you for. I know you are untruthful in some regards, but I don't know exactly how. Though our friends would trust my intuition very much, not having details, there's not much I could even accuse you of."

Mary smiled, relieved.

"And I wouldn't want to expose you," Indira said. "Because just as I said, fate has taken its own course. And I won't meddle anymore. I was trying to control things. When I saw that it wasn't going my way, I grew desperate and threatened you. I was wrong. And I am sorry."

"But what's happened? What changed to make you—"

Mrs. Singh pressed her finger to Mary's lips, quieting her.

"It's now time for you to walk alone," she said, knowingly. "Soon, you shall know everything."

The small woman turned and faded into the wispy fog that had rolled in from the lake, and Mary briefly wondered what Indira could foresee, before shaking off the sentiment and continuing her garden walk.

Indira might think the issue was resolved with her merely having stepped out of the way, but Beatrice Stallwood was still in the picture—though she was just a name. An unknown girl. Mr. Singh's fiancée, nonetheless.

Oh, why had Mary ever met dashing, mysterious, and comforting Mr. Singh? Much as she tried, she could not rid her mind of every short and seemingly insignificant encounter with him, every small and electrifying touch. Mr. Singh and his handsome physique. Mr. Singh and his deep, comforting voice. Mr. Singh and the sweet aroma of his cologne, ever so light. Mr. Singh and his dances like velvet; his dances like absolute velvet. Twirling her around like the floor was oiled for hours and hours and hours.

Somebody else's Mr. Singh.

Now, the fog was thick, but the full moon shone brightly. In the distance, at the end of the hedge row she was walking along, she spotted a figure coming her way and thought it might be Indira again, but at closer inspection, it seemed to be a man dressed in afternoon attire. For a moment she was afraid that it was either Declan with some unpleasant business or oversexed Arthur Prickwhile, either planning to grovel for forgiveness or force himself on her again. Her fears were laid instantly to rest, when captivating Mr. Advik

Singh emerged from the fog, wrapped her instantly in his strong arms, lifted her up, and caught her bottom lip between both of his.

And the mysterious energy coursed through them like never before. They positively pulsed. His lips, so plump, were soft and tasted sweet. She could not resist. She yielded to his embrace and his kiss, much more than she had during their first, sweet kiss nights before. His body was firm against hers and she melted into him, if only for a moment.

Was this really happening? And how had she let it? She had been bound and determined to not betray Beatrice, even up until this last moment. But alas, she could not be morally strong in such a situation. The temptation was far too great as was the opportunity for pleasure.

Unlike Arthur, Mr. Singh did not selfishly continue in his passion, instead he put her down and held her at the waist, distancing his face from hers enough to see her eyes. Then he swept back her curls with his right hand while he embraced her with the other. Almost immediately after the connection of their kiss was severed, Mary's familiar guilty feelings descended upon her, and a lone tear trickled down her cheek.

"Whatever is the matter? I have been bold, I know. But I have wanted this kiss for a long time. Don't tell me you have not. I wouldn't believe you."

"Mr. Singh, you are engaged to be married."

"I am *not*," Mr. Singh announced, beaming.

"But... how..."

Mr. Singh reached inside his coat pocket, pulling out a letter, a bright smile on full display. "It seems my sister sent a messenger on horseback to Beatrice yesterday in London. He brought this back. She wrote it immediately. She's as relieved to be freed as I am."

Mary unfolded the letter from Beatrice to Indira, and skimmed its contents.

... was unsure how to break the news to you, my dearest friend... wish to be engaged to a solicitor of my father's... handsome young man with a good income... very much in love... so happy to hear Advik has also found someone... could not have come at a better time...

"Oh!" Mary exclaimed, now hot in the face. Everything she'd wanted was at her fingertips. "Are you sure Indira did all this?"

"Oh, yes!" Advik laughed. "She sent the messenger as a sign—if Beatrice was sad, it was a sign to continue the union. If she was relieved, it was fate that we should end the agreement. She told me just now that her spirit discerned that you are the woman intended for me. Come."

Now, he rose to his feet and extended his hand. There in the garden, they waltzed without music among the lakeside fog under the spotlight of the full, bright moon. Their only spectators, rose bushes full of closed-up early-spring buds which would explode colorfully in the late May sun. Their only care, the freedom to relish in their love.

"Of course," he added as they twirled, "I did not need my sister to tell me anything at all. I knew you were mine from our very first dance."

He stopped the dance and kissed her again, most passionately, their two bodies closer than ever before, like two magnets clinging together. The most natural thing in the world.

"Oh." Mary sighed, pulling away, grabbing at the clothing over his chest. "We must marry soon. My passion overcomes me."

"Yes." Mr. Singh panted, and reached inside his coat pocket, drawing out an intricate gold band with a large, shining ruby. "Until something more English can be procured," he said bashfully and placed it on her finger. "I meant to give this to you this morning, but we recall how that went, don't we?"

"Is it Indian? I love it. I can tell you now, I love all of India, and I love you. I would never ask you to leave Calcutta. I can go there with you," offered Mary freely and committedly, just as Roy and Briddie may have spoken of their forevers when they first met. She feared no rejection. She held nothing back. Everything was perfectly, instantaneously right. She would meld her life with Mr. Singh's.

"Oh Mary, how I love and treasure you," he said with a quick kiss. He escorted her to the glass exterior doors of the Sunshine Room. "What if I want to leave India? Would that be a problem? Or," he thought a moment, and then looked into her eyes, "we could even go to Greece with your family."

Greece.

The word cut through the air and rang in Mary's mind, which started off with its circular, frenzied thoughts, as all of the romantic emotion of the night came tumbling down catastrophically. *I am a fraud. None of this is real. He loves a woman who does not exist. Tomorrow Mary Agnes Riboneaux ceases to be. Tomorrow I will blend into the grimy walls of The Drabbe never to be seen, or loved, again. Tomorrow this wonderful, captivating, sensual man will know that I stole a name and clothing, an invitation to the ball. He will know that I fabricated a life story. He will know that I helped steal Arthur's watch. He will know it all, and he will grieve.*

Why Mary had not thought this way before, she did not know. So consumed had she been with the perceived wrongs of her friends supporting bigamy or divorce, that she failed to see how she was allowing this grievous wrong to be done to Advik. Myrtle's words that she spoke to herself as she walked up Mannerley's long front drive that first day came to the forefront of her mind: *You must not fall in love, and you must not cause any bloke to love* you. She had allowed Mr. Singh to love her. And now, she also loved him.

How sticky, messy, awful this situation had become.

If Mr. Singh really loved her, he would need to know the whole truth. Good Friday services would be the following morning at ten o'clock. She would stay behind after breakfast with him and tell him everything instead of attending church. She did not care if Declan's plans were thwarted. She did not care if Mr. Singh turned on her and sent for the authorities. This was her one and only true shot at love, and even if it weren't her only shot, she preferred Mr. Advik Singh to any other man on the whole face of the earth. She had to take this chance and try with honesty, though it pained her and unnerved her to the core.

"My darling, what has come over your face?" Advik asked. "You seem greatly upset by something. What is it?"

"It's nothing. Your talk of Greece reminded me of something unpleasant. I will tell you tomorrow after breakfast. Will you stay behind with me instead of attending service? It might take some time."

Mr. Singh's face pinched in slight concern. "Of course, darling. I shall look forward to hearing it. As for tonight, I wanted to stroll a bit more. Will you come with me? Or shall I escort you to your room?"

"No, no. You walk. I will go up alone."

"It's probably for the better," Mr. Singh blurted, now whispering. "I might not trust myself alone with you. You have an enchanting beauty, enticing even. My bride."

Mary smiled at this intimate compliment, allowing herself to feel his attention for just a moment more before they parted ways. They shared one last kiss, and she went up to her room and twirled the ruby ring in front of the fire as she thought of what she would say to Advik the next day, and if that kiss would have been their last. The precious, sparkling gem was worth more than all her possessions combined, and probably Agnes's too.

She hoped against hope she could keep not only the ring, but more importantly, Advik's heart.

"Hand me that one," Lady Huntron said to her female attendant as the clock struck nine. "It is the last one, thanks be to the Lord. If I see one more bunny or read one more quote from Matthew... You would think they could pull quotes from all four gospels for a little variety... Where is Declan? He was supposed to be here thirty minutes ago."

She tore into the grimy envelope, reading the return address hastily. "Agnes Riboneaux? Now why would *she* write me a letter from inside the house? She could have come to my room at any time to speak to me. Indeed, I have had very few visitors, and I always love a young face."

"Yes, ma'am, you're right," the attendant said mindlessly, yawning as she tidied up the room.

Lady Huntron's wrinkled, arthritic hands unfolded the paper and as she read, her eyes grew wide, then wider, then widest.

CHAPTER NINETEEN
The Seventh Day

On the morning of Good Friday, April 17, 1870, Mary Potts put on her own dress and boots, after folding all of Agnes's clean clothes and arranging them in the portmanteau just as she had found them. She closed the suitcase and ran her fingers over the gilded letters. "What a journey we have been on," she whispered to it, "and I am grateful."

She would now go to breakfast and afterward she would tell Advik everything and hope for the best. Before she went down, she got on her knees and prayed. She figured many prayers were going up to heaven on that Good Friday, but God would still hear. Her prayer was that He would help her be honest and forgive her for her deceit, but most of all, that it would end well whatever that meant. She figured He knew best.

Up she stood, putting the ruby ring in her pocket. She also grabbed Antoinetta's image of Mannerley—her souvenir.

Mary did not want to throw Declan into prison or for charges to be pressed. She didn't even want Arthur to know about Declan's scheme. She secretly hoped that Declan could get away and find whatever it was he was searching for in Port Lazáre, or that perhaps Mr. Advik Singh, in his considerable wealth, would pay Declan himself for the watch and return it unharmed to Arthur.

Indeed, she would have to tell Advik about Arthur's excited attack on her, uncomfortable as it was, but telling him would surely let him see why Mary would be willing to do such a horrible thing to Arthur. It was not an excuse, but it *was* an explanation. He would not be surprised; he had warned her about Arthur, after all.

If Advik refused to pay Declan to get the watch back, and rejected Mary's explanations, she was fully prepared to face her crimes and punishment, though she prayed it wouldn't come to that.

She hoped and prayed she would be protected and rewarded, now that she had decided once and for all to be honest and good.

After giving one last look about the room to make sure everything was perfectly in place, and checking to see she had her few possessions, she left and locked her door for the last time and walked down the stairs and through the entryway and into the Sunshine Room. She entered initially with a big smile which faded to a reticent look of fear as she encountered a room full of people, with varying expressions, and most of them looking at her.

Standing in the middle of this tense tableau was Arthur Prickwhile himself, hands in his pockets, deep bags under his attractive eyes. He glared at Mary. Behind him, against the glass doors to the garden, Declan stood with just a hint of a malicious grin on his face. To the left of Arthur was Lady Huntron herself dressed to the T and also standing, while holding a crumpled envelope. On the far left of the room was Antoinetta, who sat on a sofa under silly Walt Corning's fat arm. She stared into the rugs, sweet blue eyes tainted with sadness. And finally, on the right-hand sofa at that end of the room, was Indira Singh looking right through Mary's soul as always, but calm and collected, as if she knew this encounter must happen. Advik also sat on the sofa, but stared out the windows into the garden, appearing despondent.

Mary froze in her spot by the entry doors to the Sunshine Room as she realized quickly that all these people were assembled to confront her. Lady Huntron wasted no time.

"Shall I read from a very interesting letter I received yesterday night?" She did not wait for Mary Potts to say yes as she adjusted her pince-nez eyewear and read, "Dear Lady Huntron, I have undergone terrible trials this past week and weekend when I was supposed to attend your springtime ball at Mannerley. It seems along the road from Hembin to Mannerley Town my money bag and travel trunk were displaced, and with it, all of my possessions, money, and my invitation. I called upon the gate at Mannerley but was repulsed by some of your workers who suspected me to be of lower class due to the sufferings I had endured, spawned by the loss of my things, sufferings which also affected my physical appearance.

"I have received word from a reliable source that the money bag was lost, but my brown leather portmanteau-style traveling trunk with gilded initials A.R. has been located and sent to Mannerley, as the invitation was inside and whomever found it—God bless them—was kind enough to forward it, suspecting me to be there. Though this week has been the most trying of my life, I am pleased to say that I was rescued by a kind soul, and I am now working under him, learning the trade of restaraunteurship and innkeeping, as I plan to acquire my own establishment and become a woman of business.

"Fearing I will be sent away again if I come to Mannerley without first receiving a confirmation from yourself, I should like to ask if I may attend Good Friday services at Mannerley Chapel with you, my lady, visit with you a little, and retrieve my trunk, before returning to Hembin on my way back to my parents' home near London. Please send confirmation, and I will travel to see you early Friday morning on the public coach. Sincerely, Agnes Riboneaux, The Drabbe Inn and Pub, Main Square, Hembin."

The words settled all around. Of course, everyone had already read the letter and had come to various conclusions. Mary would try to explain. "If you will allow me—"

"Did you or did you not steal this woman's trunk?" Lady Huntron asked.

Mary sighed deeply through her nerves. "I found it, and if you'll let me---"

"Ah! You *found* it. Yes, yes. How convenient," Lady Huntron laughed. "Actions like theft require notification to the authorities."

"Excuse me, ma'am," Indira Singh said, "but she is telling the truth."

Everyone's eyes darted to Indira. Mary couldn't believe she of all people was defending her, despite her sudden niceness during their garden walk the night before.

Indira went on, "Let her finish the tale, that we might have both sides of it."

"Well, go on," Lady Huntron said sternly. "I trust Indira's third eye very much."

Mary gathered her courage, fighting her emotions that distorted her voice and the tears that threatened the dams of her eyes. She spoke in her true accent, leaving the fancy talk behind. "I am telling the truth, as Indira says. And I will continue to tell the truth. This is my real voice, my real dress, my real boots. It's the nicest dress I have, and I wear it once a week on the days I don't work. I am a penniless, poor barmaid, but my name *is* Mary." Lady Huntron stared at Mary with droopy, serious, but intrigued eyes, and Arthur scoffed and shook his head. Advik continued staring out the window. "I had dreams when I was little. Dreams of falling in love, or being rescued from a life of work. Those dreams got harder and harder to fulfill. As I got older it became obvious that I was destined for a life of labor and poverty.

"I am not from Greece, and know nothing of the place. That was a lie I created during a panic on my first night here. I was born in Port Lazáre, you know, the place known for prostitution and gambling, thieves and swindlers. That was my home; I knew them all. My mother was one of them. So, you see, I was born in shame and destined to it. When my mother died when I was a young girl, my brother-in-law Roy Hicks took me in and raised me as his own, and let me live at The Drabbe where I work.

"My jobs there include caring for the children and the guests, and picking through the rubbish to find anything worthy to sell. Roy is my favorite person in the world. He is also the rescuer of Agnes. In fact, he has rescued many along the way. But I speak too much about this." Mary looked around before continuing and saw that Arthur was looking down, jaw clenched, and Antoinetta was now crying silently. Advik now watched her, eyes empty, mouth drawn.

She went on.

"On a Wednesday, a week or so ago, after a particularly horrid chimney disaster at my job, I met a man." Mary paused to swallow back her tears. Advik's face lifted, ever so slightly, as he watched her with solemn intrigue. "A wonderful man who charged me to never stop dreaming. And as fate would have it, even if I had wanted to stop dreaming, I couldn't. I encountered an opportunity I simply could not resist; the chance to see this man again, perhaps. This is how it happened.

"On the Thursday before the ball, I was performing my rubbish sorting duty, when I came across the traveling trunk. I did not steal it. I found it. Roy even said it found me. I am deeply sorry for what happened to Agnes, and as you can imagine, I never knew any of it. I even had to be convinced by Roy and Briddie, my sister, to take the invitation and come here. My plan was to come for one night only, not talk to anyone, enjoy things as a fly on the wall, then disappear and write the next day to Mannerley to let them know the trunk had been found. No harm done. But I did not expect to be loved by so many people so instantly, nor pressed to stay the entire week.

"It was wrong, I admit it. And I am sorry. I have enjoyed myself very much at the expense of another's suffering. I also did not expect to find wonderful friends here," Mary said, and Antoinetta looked up through her tears and smiled softly, "Nor did I expect to fall in love."

Arthur shot his eyes over to Mary and perked his pretty head up just a bit, thinking she was talking about him, but Mary looked at Advik, who had resumed his melancholy fixation on something beyond the window. "Forgive me, all of you. I used Agnes's things and her identity. But, upon my life, her things are all folded and clean in the trunk upstairs. I have left everything just as I found it. I have stolen nothing of hers, but the short time I stole her name."

"So, you are not a thief?" Lady Huntron asked with compassion in her eyes.

"No, ma'am. And if you will let me, I will leave today, return to The Drabbe, and never bother any of you again."

"Not so fast," Arthur said, his handsome face set on Mary. Antoinetta darted her vision to him worriedly from her place on the sofa. "You say you are not a thief. Does this look familiar to you?" From his hand he dangled his antique watch.

Mary's mouth fell open, and she glanced at Declan quickly, who smirked.

"So, you do recognize it. And you look at Declan. Interesting. Yesterday, when he was cleaning up a spill in my bathroom, it tumbled out of his pocket. I nearly jumped out of the bed, if not for this horrible and entirely random injury of the legs. I asked him where he got it, and he said you had obtained it and had asked him to sell it and give you the sum, and you would give him a portion of the sale."

"That's not true!" Mary shouted, incensed. "He had me steal it for *him*! You can ask anyone, even my Roy from The

Drabbe. He fired him from there for being a thief just last week." Mary was about to say that after what happened between her and Arthur in her room, she did not feel bad stealing from him, but for some odd reason, she could not bring herself to publicize Arthur's deviancy. Somehow, she still cared for him and wanted to save his pride.

"In truth, Mr. Prickwhile, Declan extorted me. He said he would tell everyone who I really was unless I stole it, and I feared being jailed. And I felt so bad after stealing it, seeing how it affected you. It nearly broke my heart. I swear it's true, and today I was going to talk to Mr. Singh and confess it all to him, and see how we might go about returning your watch to you. It was my plan, honest! But *Declan's* plan was to leave today for Port Lazáre, sell the watch, and never return again."

Arthur now paced the room among all the worried and fearful faces. He chuckled through his nose. "Interesting story, indeed. Is this true Declan?"

"No, sir."

"And were you planning to leave today?"

"No, sir. Absolutely not, sir. I am most grateful for my position, sir."

Oh, sleazy Declan, what a fawning bootlicker.

"He's lying!" Mary was growing more and more upset with each passing moment. "Please don't notify the police. I will go away and will never bother any of you again. You have your watch. No harm was done. Agnes can come here and retrieve her things. I will vanish as if I never existed."

"Indeed, a carriage was sent for Agnes first thing this morning. She will be arriving any time," Lady Huntron said. She sat wearily on an upholstered chair and thought a moment before saying, "Arthur, let us calm ourselves. You say this girl is lying, she says she is not. She says the boy server is lying, he says he is not. There is no way to test who is telling the truth, and she is right, you have your timepiece. She has been dreadfully open with all of us here, even to the smallest, most shameful detail. I do not see why we should pursue strife with someone so poor, someone who only wanted to taste our manner of life if only for a moment.

"Let us allow her to leave. Let us act like nothing has happened. In all my years, I have learned that forgiveness is the most powerful of all reactions. She has asked for forgiveness. Let us give it to her. We who have the power to do so. And today being Good Friday, after all. A day we remember the forgiveness available for our own souls."

The room fell silent. Arthur rubbed at his forehead, engulfed in thought. Then he turned his handsome face toward Mary. There was something different in his eyes; it was a similar look to the dishevelment he expressed after losing his watch. Mary tried to interpret it and wished she had Indira's sixth sense. Was it disappointment? Or longing?

No, it was love. She shivered. Poor Arthur.

He finally spoke, blurting out what he had to say quickly and without feeling, in a quieter voice than he usually used. "Mary, I forgive you. Go in peace." Declan's face distorted with shock and Antoinetta sighed audibly and relievedly.

Mary collapsed onto her knees in relief and sobbed.

"Go, I said," Arthur repeated stoically.

"Yes," she said between heavy, wet breaths, "I shall. I shall go. I would only like to address each one of you before I do. Walt Corning, thank you for the talks of pond species, most enlightening. Please be kind to your bride. Antoinetta, you have been a true and faithful friend. Thank you for sharing your world with me. I shall never forget it. Though we are in two separate classes now, and you will not care to meet with me where I live. You now know where you can find me should you ever need me. I would drop anything to help you in any way. I have loved being your friend.

"Lady Huntron, I appreciate so much your hospitality and grace. You have treated me kindly even with my erratic behavior. You are a woman full of class and your home is superb, the most beautiful in England. Even better than I had heard.

"Arthur, I have said most of what I want to say to you. I thank you for your forgiveness and mercy upon me. I forgive you as well." His face flushed with emotion. He knew exactly what she was referring to. He looked down, severing his connection with her once and for all.

"Declan, may you prove yourself worthy to work in this fine place with these fine people. Indira Singh, you are a most protective, special, and loving sister. I would have liked very much to call you my own. In fact," Mary took courage and walked across the room and knelt in front of dashing Advik Singh. She took the ring out of her pocket and held it in her open palm in front of him. He was still avoiding her eyes.

"Only one thing this whole week, besides my friendship with Antoinetta, was entirely true. I did love you, and I do love you." She paused briefly and looked back at Arthur, whose shocked face showed he had no idea that Mary and Mr. Singh had been engaged. She almost spoke to him again to explain but chose to devote her energy to Mr. Singh, the man she really loved. "You were my dream that died so long ago; the dream I gave up on little by little, until the day I found the traveling trunk that led me to you. I am sorry for it all, but I am not sorry I met you and I am not sorry I fell in love. Take your precious stone and give it to someone worthy."

Advik now turned his gaze to Mary, and she saw that his black eyes betrayed his inner pain.

"Keep it," he muttered, "it was a gift. And a gift is not to be taken back by the giver."

"It was a gift indicative of a promise. A promise that the character I was playing very much wanted to honor."

"Keep it," he insisted, closing her hand around it, sending the electric energy soaring through every part of her body, leaving her tingling all over. Her dear Mr. Singh. "Keep it," he said, one last time, in a voice near a whisper.

Mary rose and pocketed the ring. She breathed heavily in and just as heavily out. She put one foot in front of the other and walked straight out of the Sunshine Room, through the entryway and out the immaculate front doors. She passed a tall, blonde thing who was let in by an attendant and who walked unknowingly into the Sunshine Room, happy as ever, perhaps suspecting it to be a welcome party.

"Oh child," Lady Huntron said. "Sit. We have so much to explain."

As Lady Huntron's words faded, Mary traipsed down the front steps and all the way to the end of the front walk, where she was let out of the gate slow as ever, and saw her Roy waiting for her by the junky carriage, worried, and with his unkempt hair on proud display, as always.

"Mary," he said, "I came right away, following Agnes's carriage at a safe distance, as soon as I knew she was headed here. Have they let you go free?"

"Roy," Mary started, falling into his fatherly arms and weeping a bit more. "I can explain the happenings some other time. I am a mess. Take me home. I long for my small bed and the tenderness of all of those Hicks children."

"Right." Roy helped her up into the carriage. "Let's go home."

CHAPTER TWENTY

A Visitor

And so, Mary Potts returned to The Drabbe and settled back into her normal routine of life, cleaning, serving, and caring for others as she was thoroughly trained to do. Even so, her mind was not free. Whereas in the past, before her seven days at Mannerley, she was able to go about her tasks fully engaged and even enthusiastically, now she completed things out of mere duty with an empty heart and a preoccupied and sad mind, having experienced things so lovely there were hardly words for them, and then feeling the quick and painful withdrawal of these things.

The greatest and most nagging perturbation in her mind was, naturally, the question of why Mr. Singh had not written, had not visited, had not sent word. If he had loved her like he said he did, and their connection had been so strong, how could he put it all away without any further thought or remorse? How could he forget a love like that so very easily?

Months passed, summer came, and Mary Potts floated apathetically through life like a ghost; more of a ghost than Mary Agnes Riboneaux ever was.

Of course, she told Roy and Briddie everything shortly after she returned that Good Friday morning. Their take on things was that she should be grateful for at least having experienced what so few can in life. She was not so sure about all that. It seemed to her that she had put her heart through the wringer, and for very little in return. When she offered this conclusion in conversation with her sister and brother-in-law, Briddie had said that it was ridiculous; she need only sell the invaluable ruby ring and go off and make a different life for herself. That would be her recompense for the emotional suffering. A better life.

She thought about it, even seriously considered it a time or two, but could never bring herself to do it. It was the only thing she had left of Advik, and it made her feel closer to him. She did not openly admit it, but her lovesick heart longed for him day in and day out. She always expected this desire to wane, but it only grew.

One slow Thursday in late July, Mary was finishing the breakfast service in the dining room with the last straggling guests, and had just walked behind the bar to dry some dishes that Roy was washing. As she wiped methodically with her towel and stacked the plates, Roy interrupted her thoughts.

"Mary, I think you have a visitor."

She left her task and turned toward the door. There, dressed in black from head to toe, was sweet-faced Antoinetta Prickwhile, who upon meeting Mary's eyes, smiled softly and stepped toward her.

Mary could not help herself. Her heart was in her throat. She walked out from behind the bar and hugged Antoinetta, most inappropriately, and the few guests in the dining room looked on with wonder and shock. Antoinetta did not mind. When their embrace was done, she held Mary at arm's length and looked her over compassionately. "So, I guess it's true then. This is the real Mary."

"Yes," Mary said shyly. "Though you always knew the real Mary; I was always myself with you. Sit, and I shall serve you, Miss Prickwhile."

"Yes, thank you." Tired Antoinetta took a seat at the bar while Mary prepared her coffee and biscuits. "It's Mrs. Corning, now. But I want you to call me Antoinetta, like old times."

"Oh, congratulations. I wondered when it would happen," Mary said, then added, "and because of my position, I should call you Mrs. Corning. Anything else would not be fitting."

Antoinetta looked up from her cup and said in her gentle but stern way, "Call me Antoinetta, or I shall leave at once." When Mary looked at her with trepidation because of her seriousness, Antoinetta broke into a wide smile and the two laughed. Then Antoinetta remarked, "Ah, it feels very good to laugh again."

Mary then grew concerned. "Antoinetta, as it were, I notice you are dressed for mourning. Might I know the reason?"

"Indeed, and this is the very reason I have come. I have sad news. My brother Arthur is dead."

Antoinetta fought back tears at speaking the words, and Mary covered her mouth with her hand and gasped.

"When did this happen? And how? Oh, forgive me, I have lost all propriety. The details are yours alone to give, and I am not entitled to any of them. Antoinetta, I am deeply sorry because of this. Your brother loved you very much."

"Yes. Though we bickered as siblings do, he doted on me. I was the only stable woman in his life. The only one who loved him from birth till death. It happened in Calcutta last week. There was a fire in the factory on a day when only he and a few other overseers were there. The way the fire personnel explained things, due to the way the fire occurred and some evidence at the site, it was perceived to be deliberately done, perhaps by someone Arthur had wronged. I was told by the magistrates to consider his death a murder."

Her voice broke, and she dabbed at tears with a white, laced handkerchief that stood out drastically against her black satin glove. Mary had so much to say, so much to ask, but she bit her tongue. It was clear that Antoinetta had barely talked of the happenings and would want to share and be heard.

"And of course, I should not be surprised. My Arthur had many enemies. He had wronged many women, and their brothers or fathers might seek revenge. He was much too excited and vigorous in areas other than intellect."

Mary remembered well. She glanced at The Drabbe dining room's fireplace and fire poker. She still wondered what would have happened if it hadn't been within her reach. She thought about that moment often, traumatic as it was. But she always remembered the sudden compassion that overcame his voice and his slight hesitation as he asked her if she really meant that he should stop, a hesitation quick enough to give her time to severely burn his calves and thwart his attempt. Now he was burned up, dead.

He would have stopped. She knew it. Poor Arthur. He was no monster. He was merely excited, as Antoinetta defined him. Excited was the perfect term. And as soon as he got what he thought was her enthusiastic consent, he sprang into action.

"His body has been lying at Mannerley Chapel since last night," Antoinetta said. "It'll be in the paper tomorrow. The funeral is also tomorrow, Friday, July 22, at noon. I've never been fond of the month of July, you know. Bad things always happen in July.

"Anyway, all the town is coming to see him and pay their respects, though the coffin is closed. The remains were so charred, you see, as to be unrecognizable. Only three people perished in the fire. He was identified by the watch Declan tried to have you steal, which hung on his jacket pocket. It lay upon his charred bones when he was found. I'm having him buried with it. It seems like the right thing to do."

"Yes, of course. How terrible," Mary confessed. "And it *was* Declan who tried to have me steal that watch. I told the truth in that regard."

"Yes, Mary. We know. We all know. Declan was caught stealing again only days later. Agnes Riboneaux was invited to stay a week at Mannerley after Easter as a gesture for her suffering, and for our staff and my brother having repulsed her in her lowest state when she sought refuge at our gates. During her stay, she and I became friends. She is very hardworking and helpful. Certainly not as entertaining as you, but she has many pleasant qualities. We went shopping in Mannerley Town one day, and she purchased a pair of golden teardrop earrings. When they went missing a few days later, she thought she had submitted a garment for washing with the earrings in the pocket, as she frequently removed them due to their heaviness. She drove herself mad searching all over the house—nothing.

It was only a day after this that an interesting caller came to our gates saying that he was an employee from the jewelry shop in town, and he had written a letter to us explaining how a freckle-faced, redheaded young man had come in trying to sell him a pair of earrings—earrings this man had just sold to Miss Riboneaux only days before. Of course, it did not take us long to realize that Declan had done away with the letter when it came in. He was presented to the authorities on charges of stealing both Arthur's watch as well as Agnes's earrings, and unlawfully tampering with official mail and correspondence of Mannerley estate. He is in prison near London awaiting trial."

Mary sighed. "I am sorry to hear he did not make something better of his life, as I charged him."

"Indeed, Mary, your words to him when you spoke to us all before your departure were the most direct and grace-filled words he may have ever heard."

The conversation lulled, but not uncomfortably, as both of them wrapped their heads around everything. The death, the theft, Agnes, all their history together. Then Mary spoke from her heart, which beat strongly within her, nervous as she became.

"And might I know—I'm scared to ask. Mr. Singh? Is he still in England?"

Antoinetta smiled. "He purchased a cottage on the outskirts of Mannerley Town. A fine place with nice gardens and a pleasant view of the hills surrounding my own estate. He cannot be persuaded to leave. His sister Indira and her husband, Dinesh Singh, now run their businesses, which are related and intertwined with dear Arthur's and my own. Indira pressed him to return, saying it was illogical for him to stay in England. But he would not listen. So, she tried a different method and said she would reduce his income, and he said he would take the cut if she would leave him at peace. So, she was without recourse and gave up her fight.

"They drew up a contract to legalize the pay cut, as well as some stipulations—he must travel to Calcutta twice a year, among other specifics..."

Mary stared at Antoinetta as she spoke about the other elements of the contract, searching for words. Why would Advik stay in England, so far from his home, family, and businesses? And then, again, that nagging, uneasy thought that pursued her: why on earth, especially being so physically close, had he made absolutely no contact? Why had he not sent any sort of word—even a letter of forgiveness, or accusation, for that matter?

Soon Antoinetta was done, but noticed Mary was lost in thought.

"You know what, Mary?" Antoinetta started, as Roy returned to the bar to continue his preparations for the next meal service. "I have an idea. I know you won't want this, but... why don't you come with me today to see Mr. Singh? I can have you back here by evening. It is only ten o'clock now."

"Oh, no, Antoinetta. After everything that happened, I couldn't do that."

"But Mary, he is quite healed. He knows the truth now about Declan's watch, and it is my understanding that Indira instructed him to forgive you, and you know how he very much trusts his sister's word."

"Him and everyone," Mary muttered. "I just don't think he would want to see me, is all." Indeed, Mary had no reason to believe otherwise.

"Mary, it's been months. And for young folks like ourselves, months since a jilt is a whole lifetime. There is not much road traffic today. I'm sure Roy could handle things without you?" Antoinetta looked over at Roy, brow raised.

"Yes, Mrs. Corning. Indeed. Mary should go with you."

Mary looked back and forth between them. The truth was, she longed to see Mr. Singh again, even if she was a nervous wreck during the entire visit.

"But back before dinner, as you said."

"Of course. Then it's settled," Antoinetta said.

She reached for her hand over the bar, took it, and led her around the bar and into the dining room, where she locked arms with Mary and told her to take her to her quarters so they could get her changed. Mary led her through the thin hall to the inn and up the staircase to the attic rooms where her things were, and Antoinetta never once scorned the humble appearance of it.

Of course, as she walked, she furthered her explanation thoroughly. "... and you know, death opens doors and changes etiquettes. He can't hold the happenings of the past against you while facing his best friend's funeral. And you are doing me a great favor by accompanying me as I grieve my brother. I have no youthful company here and Walt is in London on business. He will be there for the funeral tomorrow but at the last minute. Lady Huntron is very upset indeed; Arthur was a pet of hers. She is so sad she has sunk into depression and is ill in bed again. It has been four times that she has been ill since spring. The doctor suspects some sort of tumor or otherwise cancerous lesion. As old as she is, it is no surprise that she suffers in this way."

Soon Mary was dressed in her nicest garments, which were still simple in comparison to Antoinetta's elaborate mourning dress. They went back downstairs, and Antoinetta loaded up in the carriage, but Mary ran inside quickly to say goodbye to Roy.

After a quick hug, she headed toward the door, but he called her name out after her, making her stop in her tracks.

"Yes, what is it?"

"Just... don't leave anything unsaid."

Mary smiled. "Yes, Roy. Especially now. For if all hope is lost, I have nothing left to lose."

CHAPTER TWENTY-ONE
The Cottage

It was just after noon when Antoinetta and Mary dismounted the carriage and stepped out onto a stone walkway among copious rose bushes, blooming with pride in all shades of pink—a walkway that led to the most picturesque cottage Mary had ever seen.

Shrouded in shady trees, the thatched cottage was made of stucco and beams, though the foundation was local stone. It was in no way poor or shabby, but it was freer, less formal than Mannerley by a long shot, and it appeared that the inside was spacious.

It was altogether lovely, and Mary stopped for a moment to take it all in. Antoinetta continued up the walkway, calling back to ask Mary what she was waiting for. It then occurred to Mary that Antoinetta had seen so much of the world, so many of the rich things and the poor things in both countries, that she was numb to becoming impressed or even disgusted by structures and decor. It was all the same to her.

Mary picked up speed and met her friend by the door just as a servant girl opened it and invited the two women inside, as it was now drizzling. They waited for just a moment near the entryway where Mary surveyed the inside. All the floors were shiny, dark wood. A staircase was in front of her, and the room to her right appeared to be a humble but well-stocked library. They were soon let into the room to the left, which was the sitting room, where there was an oriental rug and ornate wooden furniture with dark blue velvet upholstery. Crimson-colored floor-to-ceiling drapes hung near the windows, and a large, gold framed painting of a colonnaded white mansion hung over the mantle.

Mary, at first glance, thought it was Mannerley, but then realized it was an entirely different structure. All throughout the house were rich colors and the scent of spices was pleasant. And notably, there was just as much of England as of India. On the English oak table sat an ornate and steaming hot Indian tea set, no doubt prepared by the maid at the same time as every day. Along a small shelf of materials that Mary figured Mr. Singh was currently reading, or might reference a lot, were titles in both English and Bengali, some appearing medical, others not.

On a writing desk by the window among rustled papers and handbooks was both a statue of the crucified Christ and a clay form, ornate elephant. Mr. Singh must read and write in that desk chair, and do his corresponding there. The businessman, Mr. Singh, with his dances like velvet and his hair like the smoothest, blackest night. She shivered.

For a moment, the painful thought shot through her heart: why had he not reached out to her if he was so close? She tried to push the thought away, but her anxiety grew, and she whispered to Antoinetta, "What am I doing here? This is insane."

"Shh," Antoinetta whispered, "here he comes."

The two women stood to greet Mr. Singh, who walked in quickly and smiling, but stopped and wiped his face of all happiness upon seeing Mary. He looked quite shocked to find her there, but then he forced a smile and tried to seem pleasant.

"Mrs. Corning," he said and shook her hand. "Miss…"

"Potts," Mary said, blushing deeply, and fearing he could see her nervous heart throbbing through her clothes. How she longed to run into his arms as if nothing had ever come between them, to kiss his face, to feel his lips. Here he was, the object of her months-long daily fantasy; the reason she could not be truly happy, in the flesh.

"Miss Potts," he repeated, nearly whispering, and extended his hand.

She hesitated before taking it. But when she did, the same electric, magical energy coursed through them. She looked up toward his eyes to see if he felt it, too. He undoubtedly had, for his eyes were just a little wider, and his facial expression betrayed the shared experience. She was about to pull away, but before she could, he pressed the back of her hand to his soft mouth ever so slightly, like he had that first night in the courtyard at The Drabbe so long ago.

"This is a surprise," he admitted and released her.

Mary tucked in her emotions as neatly as she could, smiling politely, though every feeling in her threatened to burst forth at the slightest provocation.

He instructed them to sit, and they did so, and they were promptly served tea with sandwiches, though they ate in silence. Mary tried to eat but was so self-aware she could barely bite her food. She was thankful when Antoinetta and Mr. Singh devoted themselves to talking about Arthur's death and upcoming burial, legal issues with the business, inheritances, and such things. The conversation was dull and mournful, but at least it was not silent.

Mary rested on the sofa while they continued their talk, often focusing on the pleasant classiness of Antoinetta's gesticulations and mannerisms. She was so obviously well-bred, but not haughty. At other times, when she knew she wouldn't be caught, she glanced at Mr. Singh, with his light tan suit and vest and crimson silk cravat. His broad shoulders and manly way of sitting; a man of true military class he was. His tea-colored skin and deep, sparkly eyes, kind face, plush mouth, swept-back hair, perfect ears...

"Mary, are you quite alright?" Antoinetta interrupted her survey.

"No," Mary blurted much too quickly, glancing over at Antoinetta who stifled a chuckle at her odd behavior. "No, I need some air. Arthur's death and all. Excuse me."

Out of embarrassment she shot up and rushed out the front door to the rose-flanked walkway, beating herself up all the way. It had been true; she could not get the image of Arthur's charred body out of her mind. Poor Arthur. Given the right opportunity, with the right woman, he could have been a fabulous partner in life. Arthur dead at twenty-four.

The drizzle was barely palpable now and seemed more like a mist, but the sky looked like it could give out at any time. There, under the gray clouds, she breathed out her anxiety and hoped Mr. Singh had not noticed her erraticism. She spent about ten minutes strolling among the roses until she sat on a small iron bench off the path to admire the hills and try to calm her nerves.

"Mary."

The masculine voice came from behind her, and she craned her neck to see it was Mr. Singh looking apprehensive and guarded.

"Antoinetta is drafting an urgent legal document about ownership; you know, one of those things I'll have to send to Calcutta as soon as I can. It seems Arthur's death has complicated things. I thought I might sit out here, with you, while she completes it."

"Yes, indeed. Please. And I promise to never lie anymore, ever."

He chuckled relievedly. "Very well, then. We've been talking of business things for nearly an hour. I imagine you must be bored."

"Yes," Mary said too quickly, then tried to change her answer. "I mean---"

"Ah, but Mary, you promised to be completely honest."

He chuckled, and she couldn't help but break into a reluctant smile, too. "Then, yes, I was bored. But I was studying the room, which kept me busy." *I was studying you, Advik.* "Your home is delightful."

"Thank you."

Now, what should she say? Roy's words rang through her mind: *Don't let anything be left unsaid.* She decided to start with what Mr. Singh must be feeling.

"You must feel very upset over Arthur. I am sorry you lost your dear friend."

"It is odd to me; perhaps it hasn't hit me yet, or I haven't accepted it. It feels as if he were not really dead. As if he would trudge up the old Mannerley Town road one day and come knocking on my door. Perhaps when we bury him, I will accept it, but now it seems so absurd to me. Arthur, dead? I did cry when I found out. Of course, I am very sorry, especially to Antoinetta, but truly I cannot assimilate the fact."

"I see," Mary said, safely.

"Now that you have pledged to be honest, let me have the truth. How do you *really* feel about the spoiled little rich boy having passed away?"

Mary turned her whole body to face him on the bench and they locked gazes. "In complete honesty and transparency, I have much to say about this. Firstly, I am quite saddened by his death and cried with Antoinetta on the way here. It is awful. Secondly, I assume you mean that since I am poor, and confessed it to you all, that the whole time I hated him for his wealth. I was not that type of poor girl. I did not dislike him for being rich or privileged or any of that. Arthur lavished me with affection, even grew to love me, I believe. But I did not love him back." *I loved you, Advik.*

"Yes, I recall," Mr. Singh mumbled, in a droning, nasal way, darting his gaze and relaxedly tossing a stone across the lawn.

"Now, Mr. Singh, if you will look at me again, you will see the complete honesty in my eyes. There is something that I never told you that I should have. The watch situation with Declan—"

"Yes, I know, and we all believe you, Mary. Let us leave it in the past, where it belongs."

"No, there is more. Please look at me," she pleaded, and he turned his face reluctantly toward hers. Her eyes welled up with tears, while his remained squinted with guardedness. "You warned me of him, and I did not take you seriously. There was a confusion, a misunderstanding." Suddenly, Mary wept, hating herself for it and wishing she could control it.

"Why are you crying, Mary?" He took her hand in his, sending sparks. "Please do not torture me this way. It breaks me to see you so upset. Speak plainly."

Mary sniffled and regained a bit of composure. It was hard to confess, but he needed to know. "The confusion was that Declan had told me he was coming at a certain hour for the watch. When he knocked on the door, I thought it best I talked to him through the door where he would be forced to listen. And I told him, among other things, that I was going to give it to him and to come in and take it. Only, it wasn't Declan, it was Arthur, and he interpreted this to mean that I wanted to... that I wanted to..."

Mr. Singh gasped, horrified. "No! Did he?"

"He did attack me. He pushed me to the ground and nearly undressed me, but he did not succeed. I fought back with the fire poker, and badly burned his calves."

"Mary," Mr. Singh groaned slowly, now holding her face in his hand, and wiping at her tears. "Mary, Mary."

Then his face hardened. He removed his hand, rose, and stood a few yards in front of her with his back to her, staring out across the hills. She sat, gathering herself and wondering if she should have told him. Amidst this self-doubt and fear, he turned and walked toward her and sat again, but trepidatiously, still not giving his full self to her confidence. He was still holding something back.

"Do you know why I have not contacted you these three months?"

"Indeed, sir, I would like to know. It has been a most urgent question in my mind."

"Since we are being honest, I will tell you. I thought you were playing with Arthur and myself. I supposed you a heartless con-woman who would make men fall in love with her to play a game with them. Before Declan was caught, I thought this was done with the purpose of stealing from them or extracting items of wealth, like Arthur's watch, or the ring I gave you, for example. After he was caught, I no longer thought you were a thief, just a horrible flirt who was only playing the part for a week—it doesn't matter, right? It's just a week, then I'll go back to my old life. These rich people's hearts don't matter. I won't get caught."

"I was disappointed in you. My sister encouraged me to write you, to visit you, and I never could. I thought maybe she had lost her special intuition. How could she want me to be close to a trick-playing flirt like yourself? And now I fear you are playing with me again with sad stories like these, intent on manipulating my heart. On one hand, it kills me to see you cry. On the other hand, I know your kind. My trust is wounded, you see."

At this, Mary stood, just as sudden raindrops spattered on the pavement stones around them. "Sir, you speak as if I really were a trick-playing flirt. And I am not. What I tell you is true. Antoinetta was there."

"Forgive me. Please try to understand my distrust. After the hurt I endured. Come, it's raining." He stood, offering her his arm, but she would not take it.

"I will *not* go in, not like this. Listen to me now, everything I explained at Mannerley the day I left, and everything

I have told you now is true. I revealed everything. Completely." *Leave nothing unsaid.* "Advik, forgive me, I escape my rank, but I will call you by the name I love. Advik, my heart flutters within myself every time I see or hear of you. These months without you have been torturous for me. I still love you, Advik."

He stood looking at her for a while as the rain fell heavier and heavier, drenching them both. If she had her way, he would have kissed her and told her he loved her too, and renewed his pledge to marry her, but it did not happen that way. No, he just stared at her for a while, still apprehensive, and now a bit frustrated.

"Well, answer me this," he demanded, brow furled in apparent anger. "Do you still have it?"

"Have what?"

"The ring," he said impatiently.

Mary reached under the neck of her sopping dress and pulled out the beautiful ruby red ring that she wore on a delicate chain. He looked at it in disbelief.

"Why would you keep that? You might have sold it and financed a better life for yourself. At least a down-payment on your own dwelling or establishment."

"Advik," Mary replied, not able to tell her tears from the rain that pelted her face, "I could never sell my heart which this ring represents. Not even for all the money in the world. How you could think I could do that, really, is beyond me. Perhaps you don't know me at all, even though I have been honest after giving up my charade. At some point it would be fair to stop punishing me for my past wrongs."

Ashamed and hurt, she grabbed her heavy, wet skirts up in her arms and ran around Mr. Singh, sobbing. She loaded herself into the carriage and watched him through the small window as she tried to calm herself, her breaths forcing themselves out powerfully with each sob. He paced in the rain, until a servant ran out with an umbrella and tried to cover him with it and walk him in. He wouldn't have it and angrily shooed the person away, who reluctantly gave up their effort. He stormed back inside alone and wet.

It was about thirty minutes later that Antoinetta emerged and got in the carriage, completely unaware of the fight the two former lovers had just had. Mary made like she was tired, and Antoinetta took notice, giving her space and refraining from conversation.

As the carriage stopped at Mannerley to let Antoinetta off before carrying on to Hembin, Antoinetta stepped down and turned to Mary. "Oddest thing just happened," she remarked. "Mr. Singh positively demanded to know what Arthur did to you."

"And what did you tell him?" Mary asked nervously, sitting up tall.

"That Arthur was impulsive and attacked you and would have stripped your purity, had you not fought back with the iron fire poker."

"Oh, Antoinetta," Mary said, sighing in relief. "God bless you."

CHAPTER TWENTY-TWO
The Return of Agnes Riboneaux

After Antoinetta Prickwhile buried her brother and spent a few weeks at Mannerley, she penned a letter to her tall, blonde friend Agnes Riboneaux, telling her of many recent happenings, such as her brother's death and also about her visit to Mary Potts at The Drabbe and their lunch spent at Advik Singh's charming cottage. A most pleasant visit, she described it, despite the rain, complicated business issues, and Mary's tiredness by the end of the day.

~

When Agnes got this letter at her parents' home, she was altogether pleased to hear from Antoinetta, and wrote her back to thank her for the news, and to send her condolences, though she already knew of Arthur's death from the London papers, popular socialite and playboy as he was around the city. She also told Antoinetta that she had given her the most marvelous idea: to visit her friend Roy at The Drabbe to talk business ventures, and to finally meet this mysterious Mary Potts who had unknowingly caused her so much trouble.

Of course, now in early August, it was all a very old set of events, and it was now humorous, though in the moment it certainly was not. No, it certainly was not.

So, Agnes went and asked her father from his tall-backed reading chair where he sat sipping a cognac and petting a white, fluffy dog, if she might finally receive his promised investment. His response was what she expected, a doting and gracious yes, as he always spoiled his daughter and gave her whatever she asked when he could. So, with her money secured, she prepared for her trip.

Her father ordered the carriage from the fellow he trusted, Richard Bell. You remember, the family acquaintance who was to chaperone Agnes and her silky blonde hair at the Mannerley springtime ball.

After hearing Agnes's ordeal, Richard Bell was profusely apologetic and disappointed in himself for not having her stay at The Drabbe and return for her the next day, or at least having traveled to Mannerley himself to make sure she and her baby pink lips had made it alright. The truth was he was very interested in the underground boxing scene and there had been three big matches the weekend of the springtime ball, and on one of them he had placed a hefty bet.

As fate would have it, he won, and the odds were such that it was an incredible amount of money that he came into almost instantly. He spent a while trying to decide what to do with it, whether to save it or spend it on military or police training, so that he forgot about Agnes and her long legs. Then Agnes came home the week after Easter recounting her tale of woe and his heart broke within him. He realized he'd been too distracted to protect her. And that's when he realized he loved her.

Anyway, back to Agnes, and back inside her head. Agnes was picked up by Richard Bell around five in the morning on Tuesday, August 9, 1870. This time, she held her money bag tight in her hands the whole way and kept her trunk at her feet. Richard had shaved and smelled of flowers. She never imagined that there was a tall, dark, and handsome man behind all that beard and scraggle who was now driving her to The Drabbe. Interesting, indeed.

It took hours to get there, so naturally they made conversation along the way. Mr. Bell was very curious about Agnes, but she kept up her reserve. She had one mission and one mission only: to convince Roy that it was time to proceed.

Oh yes, you see, Agnes and Roy were kindred spirits and sudden, great friends. Agnes and Roy and Briddie had sat together several times to talk of business, and Agnes's young and hopeful belief in limitless possibilities led Roy and Briddie to dream again. That is when Roy confessed something to Briddie: he had always saved money and had hundreds and hundreds of pounds, maybe even thousands stashed away in their very own room. And one day, he promised Agnes could come, as he trusted her, and they would count the sum and do with it according to their new vision.

The three had decided together that the smartest thing they could do was to update the rooms at The Drabbe Inn to be more fashionable and comfortable, according to Agnes's fine tastes of course, and thus catch more overnight guests on their way to Mannerley. The additional revenue from these guests, along with Agnes's father's investment and Roy's hidden cash, would go to fund the purchase of an establishment in Mannerley Town that Agnes would run herself with a portion of the profits going to Roy, and Agnes had the perfect place in mind.

She had written previously all the details to Roy; she would purchase the H.A.H.A. itself, as her father had communicated with the owners, and they were looking to sell it, as they had become elderly and wanted to retire to the countryside.

When they pulled up to The Drabbe, Richard, in his bumbling way, asked Agnes if she might like to have breakfast with him.

"*Mister* Bell, I am here on *business*," she stated in staccato, a bit flabbergasted, and he had apologized. What had gotten into him, she certainly did not know.

Down she went out of the carriage with her things in tow, thanking Mr. Bell along the way, and entered through The Drabbe's main dining room door to find Briddie and Roy already setting a table to receive her for breakfast, as they had gotten her letter and expected her. Most of the guests were finishing up, and there was a pretty waitress whose black curls peeked out from under her server's bonnet who turned toward the door with a handful of dirty plates, just as Agnes said her excited hellos to Briddie and Roy. Agnes figured that must be the famous and beloved Mary Potts.

The girl smiled. Agnes smiled back. Roy and Briddie called the barmaid over a bit nervously, and toward Agnes she came. Roy introduced the two and Agnes's suspicion about her identity was confirmed. Then, Mary tore into an apology.

"I must ask for your pardon. The way I behaved—the truth is I do not know where to begin, other than to tell you I feel very badly for the turn of events that so negatively affected you."

"Oh, you are a sweet girl. I believe in fate. Do you? I think that those things had to happen for me to meet your sister and brother-in-law, and to receive my calling in life, which we will speak of today. I hope to better your lives and my own."

"Does this mean there are no hard feelings?" Mary's eyes were hopeful. She was doe-eyed, and delicate. Agnes liked her immediately.

"None at all," Agnes said confidently. "I spoke with Roy, and I understand why he kept his knowledge about the trunk from me. You are his family. I would also do anything to protect my own. And after I walked into the Sunshine Room that day, passing you along the entrance way, Lady Huntron spoke to me and explained the situation. I was only briefly upset. Lady Huntron is a woman of much class, that is why she is so loved. She reminded me that I should live a life of forgiveness, and to be like her, that is exactly what I aim to do."

"I am so grateful for that forgiveness, Miss Riboneaux," Mary replied, and Agnes sensed her genuineness. "I am indebted to you."

"Nonsense! We shall become friends, I'd say, with me living here for a while. A debt strains a friendship, and we can't have that."

"No, we can't," Mary agreed, smiling. There was still some sort of emptiness in her eyes that Agnes had hoped to quell with her full and open forgiveness. Alas, it must have been something else hidden in her heart. A man's doing, she presumed.

Without wasting any time, they all four sat and hashed out the details of their new business endeavor. Agnes would write to connections in London to send for rugs, tapestries, bedding, and furniture. The rooms would need painting, after the cracks were repaired, of course, and some window boxes with flowers might not be a bad idea.

In a matter of a few days, Agnes had melded back into her role at The Drabbe, and Roy continued teaching her everything he could to prepare her for proprietorship of the H.A.H.A. She was in her element, and quite literally living her dream.

CHAPTER TWENTY-THREE
A New Job

The updated look of the guest rooms at The Drabbe Inn had exactly the effect that Roy and Agnes had hoped: for the first time ever, The Drabbe retained so many guests on the way to Mannerley Town that they had to turn people away regularly. It earned such a reputation among the gentry, that people included a stop in Hembin in their traveling plans, and even wrote ahead to secure reservations. It was no longer merely a place to eat and sleep if you had to; it had become a convenient highway destination.

All of this, of course, meant money, and lots of it. Roy diligently saved all he could of the new Drabbe revenue, and together with Agnes's father's investment, and Roy's previous lifetime savings, the H.A.H.A. was soon purchased and renovations were made. The marble floors were polished, and the walls repainted a soft pink.

Crystal chandeliers hung high and window tapestries of purple damask accentuated the dark wood frames. New artwork was commissioned, and each room was outfitted with similar tastes to those of the guest rooms of Mannerley. It would give anyone who stayed there a taste of Mannerley's brand without being invited indoors. In fact, to Mary Potts, who had seen the renovations and helped with many, the rooms of Mannerley house and the apartments at the H.A.H.A. were easily confoundable.

The only difference was the view. From Mannerley House one could see nothing but hills and lakes and beautiful countryside. From the H.A.H.A. one could see the quaint shopping street. And of course, from the western facade of the structure, if a person like Mary looked through one of the windows, she could see a tiny, thatched cottage with a rose-flanked walkway in the distance, and sometimes a tiny man emerged and paced, or clipped flowers, or sat in thought.

It was on Thursday, September 1, when Mary was finishing some final decorations in one of the H.A.H.A.'s guest rooms, that tall Agnes came in excitedly and asked Mary to sit with her on the sofa.

Of course, she did, and Agnes's knees jutted up like a mountain from the low seat. "I have just spoken to Roy before he left for Hembin. The decision was difficult, and we had to run a lot of numbers, but they have decided to let you stay here and work for me, along with your oldest niece, Georgette."

Mary was a bit shocked, but hugged her excited and happy friend, and now employer, and made like she was pleased. She had known the possibility of her working permanently at the H.A.H.A. was on the table, but the truth was, it was hard being so close to Mannerley; and being so close to the cottage with roses in the distance. It wasn't the cottage, of course, but the dweller therein.

She was still miserable over Mr. Singh, especially with how they had fought at their last encounter with him accusing her of playing with men out of cruelty. She did not understand how his eyes could look at her with a longing love, but in his heart, he still held things against her. She had confessed all, and had thus decided that if he held rancor within him, it was his fault, not hers. This thought freed her, in a way, though she could not forget him. He infested her thoughts. And of course, later that day, when Agnes offered for her to choose from all the servant rooms on the highest level, she found that all of them had a window that framed Advik's little cottage. So naturally, she chose the one that best did so.

~

And so, Mary Potts' life had taken a step up, and in the end, it was without the help of a husband. She, Roy, Briddie, and Agnes had accomplished it all on their own. Instead of a crusty, poor barmaid, she was a hotel receptionist, dressed better than she ever had, and making more money, too. And she was happy with her position. She had two days off per week, and would spend them perusing the shops of Huntron Avenue, sometimes buying something for herself or Georgette, her niece of ten years, who was now in her charge.

Georgette had brown hair and freckles and attended school most mornings. She trained for all manner of work from serving, to cooking, to cleaning for a few hours each afternoon. She was paid symbolically, as Roy was adamant she was not to be forced to work, or seen as an employee. Rather, he wanted to give his oldest daughter a chance to dream as Mary had. A chance to be near Mannerley and well-bred people. And a chance to learn a trade and not be stuck with tons of babies, though he loved his own.

Georgette traveled back to Hembin every Thursday night and returned to Mannerley Town every Sunday night. It was after several of these rushed trips back and forth ......in late September and her busy school and training schedule, that Mary realized that her niece had grown pale and developed a cough. Naturally, this detail comes about, because what is a Victorian-era novel without a sick and ailing child?

The symptoms persisted for weeks, and it worried Mary, not only for her niece's health, but also because the Mannerley autumn ball was approaching, and it would be their busiest weekend since acquiring the property. They needed all hands on deck, and Georgette would need to take on many extra responsibilities instead of going home to The Drabbe. The girl said she was more than willing, but Mary wondered if she could push through.

It was on Wednesday, October 5, 1870 when Mary saw Mr. Singh again, other than spying on him through her window, far in the distance, pruning his bushes.

It was one of her days off, and she had just visited the apothecary in town to inquire about Georgette's cough, and had purchased the recommended concoction, paying, and carrying the typical glass bottle in her hand as it would not fit in her silk purse. Her large floral hat almost obscured him from view as she passed him on her way back to the H.A.H.A. that evening, but she stopped when she heard a masculine voice say, "Miss Potts."

"Yes?" she replied and turned on her heels, seeing Advik. All the color she had flew to her face. She must have matched the deep rose, high-buttoned dress she wore.

"You look well," he remarked, tenderness in his eyes, a slight smile on his lips.

"Thank you. As do you," she said politely, not forgetting her pain.

"So, the medicine is not for you?"

"No, sir. It's for a worker, my niece. She stays with me from Monday to Thursday. She must get well, for the ball is this weekend. I work at the—"

"Yes, I know," Advik interrupted, happily. "How pleased I was to hear it. I have strolled by several times. Seen you inside. I should have had the courage to say hello."

"Yes, you should have." They looked at one another for a moment in silence.

"Mary," Advik started, eschewing formalities, and taking a step closer to her. "Are you going to the ball?"

She smiled tiredly, remembering her dances with him. "I was invited by Antoinetta, but the business is new. I couldn't leave it. There is too much to be done."

"But could you not escape for a few hours? Perhaps you could..." he paused and seemed suddenly very vulnerable. "Well, perhaps you could go with me?"

Her heart beat excitedly. How handsome and how sweet he was. But she could not ignore the pain inflicted. She had to be strong. Against her will, she decided to play tough. "I could not, Advik. I only play with rich people's hearts when I think I won't get caught, or something like that which someone once told me."

The hope in his face drained to emptiness as she turned and walked straight back to the H.A.H.A., flushed redder than any field poppy ever was.

She rushed in and pushed the door closed behind her, resting on it with her eyes closed, breathing deep, trying to calm her nerves. Agnes startled her from behind the counter. "Well, I'm glad I'm not the only one upset today. You will not believe what just happened to me. Richard Bell—yes, you know, my driver. He's just come in, saying he was here on a small holiday from the police academy, and he wanted to check on me and see the business. I said very well, but then he asked me to the ball. Why on earth would he do such a thing? Doesn't he know I am dreadfully busy? He must think I'm still that daddy's money, carefree girl from back near London. Heavens, I do *not* understand that man."

Agnes fanned herself, and Mary took strength, smiled, and walked past her friend on the way to the stairs, grabbing her shoulder and saying, "It's because he's in love with you." Of course, Agnes squawked and gawked in disbelief, but Mary had already run up the stairs to her room, to replay Mr.

Singh's precious face over and over and over, and perhaps, if she were lucky, catch a glimpse of him walking his lawn, ever so tiny, off in the distance.

CHAPTER TWENTY-FOUR
The Night of the Ball

Saturday, October 8 arrived and with it, all the fancy guests to the Mannerley Ball. Mary Potts, Agnes, Georgette, and any other available workers at the H.A.H.A. scrambled to and fro checking people in, running errands, or helping the guests with last-minute needs.

Early in the morning, the requests had already begun. A woman who had checked in Thursday had just tried on her dress and it was much too tight. Good thing Agnes knew a seamstress. Another pair of gentlemen had misplaced their invitations, so out ran Georgette with official H.A.H.A. to Mannerley correspondence, asking for written permission for the men to still attend, after the guest list was checked for their names, of course. A couple had run out of firewood in their room, and another wanted to take tea early, so they could be hungrier for Mannerley's evening hors d'oeuvres. Mary took on tasks energetically, completing them one by one.

The day sped along in this way and finally, finally around half past five in the afternoon there was a lull in the work, as if an angel flew by, forcing everything and everyone to take things a little slower. What a phenomenon it was. Mary was wiping the reception desk's glass top, Agnes was rechecking the guest log, and Georgette was cleaning up someone's afternoon coffee on a small table in the lobby, when they realized the change, and Agnes was the first to comment on it.

"Look around you, ladies." Agnes sighed, taking off her glasses and placing her hand on her hip relaxedly. "It seems our hard work is done. No need to rush anymore, thank heavens."

Mary finished her task and stretched her back. "I've been at this for ten hours straight, and poor Georgette even more. What do you think of all this, Georgie?"

At this Georgette, who was walking toward the kitchen with the dirty coffee time dishes, smiled limply and said something about how it was quite alright, when her face went tragically pale, and she collapsed onto the floor in an exhausted heap of apron, dress, and messy brown hair.

Mary and Agnes screamed her name and ran to her, holding her head upright, lightly smacking her face, dribbling her with water. To Mary's relief, the child was breathing and did come to, but was terribly hot to the touch and her lungs labored heavily, much more than was normal. She took her up to her bed, which was in an adjoining room to Mary's, and sat with her there, thinking surely a thing this young could bounce back with vigor after a short rest. By a little after seven o'clock in the evening, it became clear that they needed a doctor's opinion, as she was none better.

Agnes and her long legs sprinted along Huntron Avenue, taking a left on Masquerade Street and down a few houses where she knocked ferociously on Doctor Harring's door just as the sun was setting. A maid answered.

"I need to see Dr. Harring. There is a sick child," Agnes said, winded.

"I'm very sorry but the doctor is attending the birth of twins, and as I understand it is very complicated. He came by for a quick bite to eat not long ago and said not to expect him till morning. Have you tried the apothecary?"

Of course, Agnes had already run off in despair by the time she heard this question. She jogged back to the H.A.H.A. and up to Mary and Georgette.

"Nothing?" Mary asked.

"He's at a birth," groaned Agnes, with great sadness and defeat in her eyes.

The two thought a while and Mary looked at Georgette closely, brushing the hair from her face. "Stay with her, Agnes. I know exactly who to ask."

~

It was not easy for Mary to humble herself and do what she was doing, but here she found herself entering into Mannerley's gates, shrouded in the evening darkness and a violet cloak, with trembling hands and her heart pounding. When she entered the great home, a staff member flitted off, presumably to find Antoinetta for her; they knew Mary by now, of course, friend of Antoinetta's and occasional visitor as she was.

Sweet Antoinetta, this year dressed in a luxurious chocolate brown, emerged quickly from the dance into the foyer and took Mary's hands. "Mary, you're not dressed for a ball."

"I'm afraid I have a problem and must steal one of your guests." Just then Advik Singh in full evening attire, black suit, and all, came out of the hubbub of the ballroom and stood behind Antoinetta. His eyes met Mary's with that familiar longing look.

"Advik," Mary said, forgetting titles, forgetting her place. "I must take you from this dance that you love so much. I am sorry, but my little niece is sick. She collapsed, and the doctor is on a call at another residence. I don't know who else to ask."

"There is no reason to be sorry, Mary. I shall go with you at once."

To her surprise, he wrapped his arm around her cloaked shoulders protectively and the two walked together briskly in the dark, side by side, his heat extending into hers pleasantly, as the night was cold. Of course, the mysterious energy visited them again, as it did with any contact. They did not say much, other than Advik remarking that he would give up even the best of dances to help Mary with anything at any time.

They reached his quiet, dark cottage around half past eight, and he opened the door quickly, sending a servant to get the horse. Mary watched from the entryway as he fetched a book and a small leather bag of what she assumed were medical supplies, and to which he added a few more flasks and devices quickly. Then he led Mary to the horse and sat her on it, sidesaddle, and then he got on as well, straddling her body from behind. Off they went at a comely canter until they arrived at her place of work. Mary almost fell while dismounting, she was not sure if from clumsiness or fear for Georgette, or even the lightheadedness experienced because of riding pressed against Mr. Singh's solid and masculine chest. Mr. Singh caught her effortlessly, setting her on her feet again, and tying up the horse.

"It's my nerves," she admitted and led the way up the stairs to Georgette's room.

"And also the exhaustion. I saw it on your face," Mr. Singh said from behind her as they ascended. Though she shouldn't have been concentrating on such things while her niece lay languishing, she found herself wondering if he was allowing his eyes to focus on her slender back and pleasantly protruding bustle as he climbed each step right behind her.

Once with his patient, after setting his things on the floor and dismissing Agnes, he listened to her carefully with a stethoscope and palpated her belly. He checked her tongue, eyes, and ears by candlelight.

"What tonic did you give her?" he asked, and Mary brought the bottle. "Well, we shall try something different: Ayurveda."

"I don't think I have any of that here," Mary said in all seriousness.

Mr. Singh chuckled through his nose and looked at her endearingly. "No, Mary. Ayurveda is ancient Indian medicinal knowledge. I have recently been studying it more closely, though I've dabbled in it all my life. This girl has pneumonia, but it is not bad. I believe she collapsed from exhaustion due to her condition. The tonic you have is mostly sugar water; it will do nothing to stop the infection. So, we shall try another way."

Mr. Singh sat his bag on the desk in Georgette's room and took out small vials of brightly colored powders, smelling them to determine their use. He took out a mortar with a pestle, a large glass bottle, and a sieve.

"Mary, fetch me some warm water, honey, and garlic if you have it."

Mary went as fast as she could while carrying her candle, and once in the kitchen after lighting the lamp she made much better time. She scooped warm water from atop the stove into a jar, then took the whole ring of garlic bulbs as she did not know how much he would need. There was no honey left after such a busy business day, or at least she could not find any in her nervous haste, so she took the sugar.

Up she went to Georgette's room, where Advik took the supplies and mashed a few peeled cloves in his mortar, mixing them with his spices to make a paste. One of the spices was bright yellow.

"We usually add this spice to milk," he commented to her as he poured it in. He then mixed his yellow paste with the warm water and dissolved the sugar. "The sugar is only for taste, though honey would lend sweetness and also heal the throat and fight sickness."

He then let the mixture sit for several minutes while Mary paced by Georgette's bed nervously, and after he determined that it was ready, he left the bulk of it in the bottle, but strained a portion of it into the mug, taking it to Georgette and asking Mary to help her sit up to drink.

The girl weakly held herself up, complaining of cold, and Mary supported her while she drank the concoction. Then they laid her back down and stoked her fire.

"What now, Mr. Singh?" Mary asked.

"Now we wait," he answered, and patiently packed up his supplies. "If she is better by morning, she will continue to improve. If she worsens, the doctor will need to be called, as soon as he is rested from his other call."

CHAPTER TWENTY-FIVE

By the Fire

Mary had told Mr. Singh she could handle things, not really meaning it of course. She said this more out of a desire to not further encumber Mr. Singh's evening out, but in reality she was still worried about her niece and was not confident that she could follow the correct signs to see if she was healing from her infection or not. To her great relief, he refused to leave his patient and walked through the adjoining door into Mary's chamber and said, "Oh, there are embers here. Let's build up the fire. It's cold."

Mary went into the dark room too and shut the adjoining door behind her so little Georgette could sleep. They were now alone. While Advik added more logs, which promptly crackled and illuminated the space, Mary laid a few pillows and blankets on the rug and sat resting her back on the foot of her bed, taking in the fire's warmth. Advik turned around and did a quick survey of the space.

"Oh, there's a bed there. I mean nothing by this, Mary. I hope you know that."

"Not to worry, Mr. Singh," she said. "This is my personal room."

"I just mean that considering your experience, you may think men..."

He did not finish his sentence; it just kind of fizzled away, and he sighed. He sat beside her on the rug and loosened his cravat and removed his coat.

"Mary, I was wrong," he blurted out, staring into the flames, dark eyes glowing with the reflection of firelight.

"Yes, Advik," she said. "Yes, you were."

"Forgive me," he said. "Specifically, forgive me for accusing you. You are no trickster, no flirt. I know better than that. I had seen many times the way Arthur finagled his way into a woman's life, and then her bed. It was his doing, not yours, though he did care for you especially. I had never seen that from him before."

Mary was instantly healed in so many ways after hearing his apology, but she did not let her guard completely down yet. She was still unsure how he viewed her, romantically speaking, and she did not want to mess up the delicate dance of courting and love by being too forward. Plus, she was dreadfully tired and fighting to stay awake in order to experience the wonderful things he was saying, things she had yearned to hear for a very long time.

"In a way, that makes me feel better. Knowing I wasn't merely another plaything. It makes a woman feel special, even though I did not love him back."

"I'm sure that makes you feel better. It's awful to feel like someone's plaything, especially when your heart gets involved, though yours was not. Allow me to explain myself, so you might see why I came to accuse you in that way. When you wanted *me*, and said yes to *me*, I was enamored, obsessed even. I was ready to pledge it all to you. And then the truth came out, and I felt fooled. How could I be so smart, but become so hurt? I was scrambling to make sense of it: Arthur's watch, the ruby ring, and you saying you had intended all along to disappear and return to your old life.

"My mind tried to fit you into a neat little category to scientifically explain my pain. The category I came up with was a man-eater; she must play with rich men for fun, I thought, and sometimes for gain. But it wasn't true."

"I accept your apology, Advik. And I appreciate your explanation. You have come to the correct conclusion, none of what you thought was true."

"Mary," he almost whispered, at first trepidatiously. Then he took courage, looking in her eyes, and rushed on. "Even now during my apology and explanation, I have a hard time understanding why you would allow so much flirtation from Arthur—other than his attack on you—and entertain so much affection from myself, if you knew you'd leave."

Oh, now came the hard part. Through her exhaustion, she let the words flow forth. The truth was that she didn't even understand her own answer to his question, and feared it wouldn't satisfy. She had acted irrationally and wrongly, and only truth and openness could fix things now.

"Mr. Singh, I can only say that I am sorry. This all started as a silly adventure, and I never intended to hurt anyone. As for Arthur, he never asked permission to show me affection, and everyone always paired me with him because he doted on me so, which gave him more ability to do those kinds of things. The only way to not hurt Arthur would have been to love him back, and that I could not do.

"As I've told you before, I loved you. The *real* me loved you; so much that I forgot the charade and really dreamed of being with you forever, especially after I found out Indira was merely your sister. And that is my fault. I lost control of my game. I should have protected your heart and ignored you, but I could not. Everything in me wanted you. And I will tell you one thing, I was also hurt."

"You were?" he asked from his spot beside her.

Mary's fatigue overcame her. She slid onto the floor and rested her head on a pillow to address him as she reclined.

He did the same, and they stared right into each other's eyes from their places on the rug by the fire.

"Of course, Advik. How could I not be? I got hurt when I lost you and the engagement. It killed me to break your heart; the way you looked out that window. I was hurt when I saw the pain in Antoinetta's and Arthur's eyes. I was ashamed, embarrassed. I was horrified when I learned what happened to Agnes. Really this whole thing has been a lesson in suffering for me. I don't know why you can't see that."

"Hmm," he said, eyelids growing heavy. "Perhaps I haven't tried." Then he paused and thought. "The story you told me about Arthur's attack, which Antoinetta later corroborated, made me see things very differently. I imagine you must have despised him after that; it would be very easy to play someone and steal from them if you hated them."

"Exactly," Mary said, "but it was still wrong. And I regret it. I am glad nothing came of it. And I wish you had told me all your realizations sooner."

"If I am honest, I walked by the H.A.H.A.'s front window many times with plans to go inside and explain myself and apologize. Plans to say these exact words."

"Why didn't you?"

"Something was always going on. You were always busy. You are a businesswoman now; independent. I felt foolish, embarrassed. And with how we fought in my garden, I thought you wouldn't want to see me anyway. I figured I had ruined things with my anger."

"Mr. Singh," Mary sighed and extended her hand to hold his, "I *always* want to see you." She closed her eyes.

"Mary Potts, I want to see you, always," he whispered, but it was not heard. Mary had fallen into a deep sleep as soon as her lids had shut.

Mary woke groggily and heard the Mannerley Chapel bells tolling four o'clock and the low voices of partygoers in the street, returning to their rooms to sleep off the merriment. She was now in her bed, tucked in and warm. She wondered for a moment if it had all been a dream, that was, until she shot up and peered over to see handsome Advik lying on the rug in front of the fireplace, covered and sleeping deeply, his back facing her.

She hopped down and knelt beside him and whispered his name. It was thrilling to be next to his warm, solid body as he slept. He rustled from sleep and smiled at seeing her. Then he sat up, too, and said, "I think we should check Georgette's progress."

The two tiptoed into Georgette's room. Mary worked on her fire, and Advik listened to her thoroughly with the stethoscope. He checked her for fever and timed her heartbeat and breaths. He roused her just for a moment to drink another serving of the strained herbal liquid, and afterward she turned over into her covers and sighed and fell right back asleep.

Mary watched from her place by the fire, as Advik came toward her, removing his stethoscope from his neck, a pleased smile on his face. How sweet he looked in his elegant attire among the orange glow of the fire; his shirt unbuttoned at the top, cravat loosened, sleeves rolled up, dark hair in turmoil. "She will recover," he said quietly. "Little, if any, fever. Her breathing sounds excellent, compared to last night. It was exhaustion. There is no need to call the doctor, just let her rest for several days, and have a servant wait on her. She is young and will improve very quickly."

"Oh, thank you, Advik." Mary was overjoyed that Georgette's condition was not serious. Relief flooded her mind, but also worry; she did not want Mr. Singh to leave. And now he was packing up his things quietly, slowly, as if searching for a reason to stay. And Mary could also think of no reason at all. The logical thing for him to do was leave and go home to rest. But she could not bear to be separated again.

He walked into her room, and her heart fluttered. She followed him in and shut the door.

"My suit jacket," he said, grabbing it from its place near the fire, putting it on, and then taking his leather medicine bag in hand again. They looked at one another.

Leave nothing unsaid.

"Mr. Singh," Mary blurted out impulsively, stepping in front of him on his way to the main door of the room which led to the hallway, the primary exit.

"Yes, Mary?" he asked, stopping, now close to her, looking down into her eyes.

"Do you remember," Mary stammered, nervous, "how I promised to be honest?" Now she was really risking her heart again. But she must try one last time, come what may. It was all or nothing now.

"Of course."

"Well, in all honesty, I do not want you to leave."

A sweet look swept over his face, and he smiled slightly. He set his bag on the ground and took both of her hands. The electric waves circled through them, binding their hearts to one another. He slowly, but confidently raised her hands to his plump lips now shadowed by one nights' dark stubble. He kissed every one of her knuckles, and each kiss was like a shock through Mary's heart.

"If *I'm* honest," he whispered, "I never want to be apart from you again."

He found her waist and pulled her to himself, and there he held her against his chest, as his hands traveled slowly up and down her back. Their faces brushed, their noses touched, and then their lips, meeting like the sweetest dance, over and over and over. Then he gently pulled away.

"May I?" he asked, and then reached behind Mary's curls for the delicate chain. He tugged it until the ring emerged freely from the bodice of her work dress. He removed the ruby ring from the necklace and took Mary's hand and placed it proudly on her finger, kissing it afterward.

"This time it is not to be undone. I want you to marry me and live with me and become Mary Agnes Singh. What do you say?"

"Yes, Advik!" Mary beamed. "Only, I will be Mary *Margaret* Singh."

At this, they both laughed, and continued in the comfort of each other's arms for a great while.

CHAPTER TWENTY-SIX

Happiness

So, this is where Mary's whirlwind story comes to a close, for now. Our sweet and entertaining Mary Potts was wed to dashing and handsome Advik Singh on Saturday, October 15, 1870, with a celebration afterward at Mannerley estate itself, hosted by Antoinetta Prickwhile and attended by a number of guests. Some of those in attendance you have come to know already, such as Walt Corning, Lady Huntron, who had gotten well just before the wedding reception, thank goodness, and Roy and Briddie.

Even Agnes Riboneaux was there, happier than ever that her grave misfortunes had resulted in true love and marriage, though she regretted bringing Richard Bell as her wedding date, since he pined after her like a lovesick puppy. How could a businesswoman expect to excel with a man so sentimental, so cuddly, so needy?

Advik Singh's sister Indira, who was in England already for the autumn ball, stayed in town for the wedding celebration with her husband Dinesh, and when she approached Mary in the Sunshine Room after the wedding, she smiled, sweetly and relaxedly.

"Now, you smile freely," Mary said to her. "Why is that?"

"Oh, Mary. There is no longer any deceit in you. That is why I am glad now to call you my sister. And I have something for you." She set a small package on the Sunshine Room tea table, took out a jewel, applied some adhesive, and ever so gently pressed it to Mary's forehead. "You are a married woman now. You can wear your bindi, just like Advik envisioned. He shall think you very beautiful indeed."

Mary was excited to honor Advik's vision of beauty by wearing a bindi, and she also felt identified with her mother, who when telling fortunes would wear an elaborate bindi-like headdress from her own gypsy culture, which was rumored to have originated in India. The small jewel was like a connection to her mother on the most important day of her life—her wedding day. And Indira probably had no idea how much it meant to her.

On second thought, perhaps she *did*.

"Oh, Indira, thank you." Mary hugged her new sister-in-law.

After the reception was completed, Mary returned with Advik to his home, now her home, to begin their life together. And the next day, they took their honeymoon to India. On their way, where else would they take an extended stop but Greece?

~

Antoinetta spent several days cleaning up after the party. She wasn't rushed, she did it contentedly, still abuzz from the wedding festivities. It was on her last cleaning day, while moving furniture back in place with Agnes, that something caught her eye.

"What's this?" Antoinetta asked, as she approached it.

"I don't know," Agnes said, perplexed, and came over to see.

There, near the hearth, glimmering in the firelight, was Arthur Prickwhile's antique, golden pocket watch.

Look for the next book in the series, *A Telephone at Mannerley*, in the fall of 2025.

It's December 1879, and Mary longs to rekindle things with her one true love, Mr. Singh, after their marriage has grown stale. But soon she's distracted as she finds herself playing matchmaker for an unknown-to-her younger brother, and saving Mannerley estate from being passed onto imposter heirs.

Author Bio

Audrey has always written stories. Her very first picture book which she wrote in early elementary school was about a mean, grumpy tooth fairy. Her first "novel", bound using a cardboard cereal box, was written in the fourth grade. By high school, she was writing secret novels of her own, usually naming her characters by her own initials. By her twenties, she knew that writing was her calling—and she's so glad you're reading her debut romance!

Audrey lives in North Carolina with her Spaniard husband and two young sons, is completely bilingual in Spanish, and enjoys church, crochet, jigsaw puzzles, time with friends, yoga, and funny movies. She's a freelance fiction editor on Upwork, an editor at a literary agency, and hopes to become an agent soon.

You can learn more about Audrey by visiting audreylancho.com and signing up for her newsletter—she promises

not to spam you; she'll just inform you of big happenings and new releases. Audrey also enjoys connecting with readers and other authors on X/Twitter and Instagram (@audreylancho) and would be grateful for a kind review of this book and any positive mentions on social media. Readers can connect with Audrey at
www.audreylancho.com/connect.

A Letter from Audrey

Thank you so much for reading *Seven Days at Mannerley*. I truly hope you enjoyed it. Mary's story isn't over yet, so be sure to sign up for my newsletter on my website to keep up with new releases. I won't spam you—I'll just drop a note from time to time about happenings in my author career, plus insider freebies like recipes, short stories, giveaways, in-person event details, and more!

You can sign up at audreylancho.com/connect or scan the QR code below to access my newsletter, blog, and website links, as well as my social media platforms. Be sure to give me a follow so we can keep in touch!

If you enjoyed *Seven Days at Mannerley*, there are a few ways you can support me as an up-and-coming author. Please leave me a review on any retailer, Goodreads, or other reviewing sites. I also welcome mentions on TikTok, Instagram, X, and other social media. Also, you can tell your friends to read my book. Word of mouth both online and in person is so important for new authors.

Warmly,
Audrey

P.S. Did you find the Spain and Southern USA easter eggs in the text, as well as all the names that start with A?

Acknowledgements

A book has one author, but many contributors, who deserve a hearty thanks.

Thank you, God, for opening doors and being so good to me. I don't deserve it, but I sure do enjoy it!

A special thank you to Jonathan Lancho for all your sacrifice to care for the kids so I could write. For believing in my dream. For doing everything you could to make it happen. For letting me quit my teaching job to raise our boys and write. For sacrificing a certain standard of living so I could give it one last good shot. For once, you were not practical or pragmatic, but I love you so much for it. For loving me more than anyone else and embracing our path. You are my greatest adventure.

Thank you to Alastair, for your nightly prayers for Mom's book to be published—God answered them! Thank you to Ander for taking gloriously long naps, allowing me to write all through your baby and toddler years—I couldn't have done it without you!

A very special thank you to my agent and friend, Colleen. I owe you so much for everything you've done for me. I love the trust we've built and I'm so excited for this to be the first of many deals together.

Thanks to Mom, my first beta reader. You have been with me the longest on this journey, since you knew about it from the get-go. Your enthusiasm about this book and your texts with things that remind you of my characters make me so happy. Thank you also to David, for believing I could do this and for your constant support.

Thanks to Dad, for getting so excited and for wanting this so badly for me. For when you told me that you didn't take the baseball scholarship and you always wondered what would have happened if you had. You encouraged me to give it a fair shot, to at least be able to say I'd tried. Your decision from so many years ago was not in vain—it spurred me on to follow my dream. In the end, sports grit and author grit are of the same breed. Thank you also to Ila for always, and I mean always, cheering me on.

Thanks to so many other family members (siblings, aunts, uncles, cousins, and more) who have been so genuinely excited for me, including but *definitely not* limited to, Trey, Molly, Zoe, Grammy, Grandaddy, and of course, Nanny, Agnes Schuyler, who is with the Lord, but was the first to tell me I should be a writer—and now her name is in a novel!

Thanks to my wonderful family-in-law in Spain for all their enthusiasm. They've been a source of support on hard days and encouraged me to keep pushing, and not compromise my standards or goals.

To my enthusiastic friends who've cheered me on. To those special friends who asked me, "How's your book coming?" when I was feeling like a total fraud due to having nothing to show for all my efforts. To my main group of girlfriends especially, as well as their husbands, who've seen me giddy and impatient, and been there the whole time. Thanks to my Sunday morning life group friends who've heard me whine about this for years. To friends in our hometown community who ask me and support me, and friends from other nooks and crannies of the world who have cared. You're all so wonderful!

Thank you to dear friend and mentor, bestselling romance author Cindy Holby, for believing in me, reading my first (terrible) manuscript, being honest, and critiquing my work. Thanks for looking at this first chapter early on, as well. Finally, thanks for binge-reading my novel, loving it, and giving me a quote, which I treasure. Your support and advice mean the world to me. I wouldn't be where I am without your guidance. I hope to repay you all the favors.

To Mel Ellis for beta reading—thank you! To young adult romance author Brielle D. Porter for beta reading, blurbing, and catching that contrived plot point that went on too long.

Thank you to Dawn at Vinspire for taking a chance on this debut author and all the guidance, and to my editor, Kassy Paris, for walking me through the process and for your friendship.

Find Your Next Favorite Book at
Vinspire Publishing!

www.vinspirepublishing.com

Like us on Facebook at
www.facebook.com/VinspirePublishing

Follow us on Twitter at
www.twitter.com/vinspire2004

Follow us on Instagram at
www.instagram.com/vinspirepublishing

Printed in the USA
CPSIA information can be obtained
at www.ICGtesting.com
LVHW041947010324
773322LV00006B/100